Also by Hannah Roberts McKinnon
Franny Parker

The Properties of Water

The Properties of Water

HANNAH ROBERTS MCKINNON

Farrar Straus Giroux   •   New York

Distributed in Canada by D&M Publishers, Inc.
Printed in September 2010 in the United States of America
by RR Donnelley & Sons Company, Harrisonburg, Virginia
Designed by Natalie Zanecchia
First edition, 2010
10   9   8   7   6   5   4   3   2   1

www.fsgkidsbooks.com

Library of Congress Cataloging-in-Publication Data
McKinnon, Hannah Roberts.
    The properties of water / Hannah Roberts McKinnon.— 1st ed.
        p.   cm.
    Summary: When her older sister, Marni, is paralyzed jumping off the cliffs into
the lake near their house, twelve-year-old Lace feels responsible for the accident and
struggles to find a way to help heal her family.
    ISBN: 978-0-374-36145-7 (alk. paper)
    [1. Paralysis—Fiction.]   I. Title.

PZ7.M4786847Pr 2010
[Fic]—dc22

2009041618

For Finley,
pure joy

The Properties of Water

The Jump

They awaken me. The boys' shouting is loud and playful, echoing across the water. There are two voices, both young. I pull the pillow over my head, but the voices grow, followed by a splash.

"Don't be a baby," yells one. It's some kind of dare. "Go on, jump!"

There is no response. I hold my breath because I know. I know what's about to happen; I can picture it. He is standing on the edge of Turtle Rock, just above the shore. In my mind I see him peering down, over the steep rock face, where the water is black and endless below. And I imagine him fall. The fall is slow and he's twisting in the air, arms reaching back to the rock that disappears above him. And then it isn't a boy at all, but Marni who I imagine. Her long legs point to the water, brown hair trailing above her in the speckled afternoon light. She doesn't scream, just smiles and drops until she disappears below the black surface. My stomach turns, and I lurch upright in bed.

"Jump! Jump!" The other boy's voice pierces the morning outside my window. Then, above it, there is another noise. A shriller, urgent scream shatters the quiet of my house. It is loud and fearful and I cover my ears. My bedroom door flies open, and then I realize the scream is my own, coming from my throat, raw and jagged, and I cannot stop. There is a fumble from beneath my bed as Cinder hops onto the covers, tail thumping nervously, worriedly. He woofs, and Dad descends on the bed behind him, scooping me up, pulling me in.

"Lacey, it's all right, honey, it's all right."

The voices outside have stopped, probably in wonder. "They're going to jump," I whimper into Dad's nightshirt. He sits back, his hair rumpled from sleep.

"Who? Who's going to jump?"

"The boys outside. Tell them, tell them not to!" Tears are sliding down my cheeks, and Cinder licks them away. He's wiggled in between our hug, and Dad rubs his black ears.

"Lace, those boys are okay. They're only playing."

"We have to stop them," I cry, but Dad doesn't move. He just rocks me, and Cinder presses his nose on my lap until the lake goes still outside my window.

The Lake

When Mom and Dad first came to this lake in Maine, they say they knew it was for them. They settled in Saybrook, where they found a little clapboard house with a big back porch, perfect for a family. Almost all of the pictures on our parlor wall are of this lake and us. There's one of Marni as a one-year-old, tottling on the sandy shore. There's another of me grinning at the camera and Dad sticking out his tongue, the lake looming behind us. And there's one of Mom in a red bathing suit, laughing, with Marni and me hanging on to her brown legs. I must have been five and Marni seven. The lake is everywhere, soaking our beach blankets, sucking our toes, suffusing the air we breathe. Growing up on this lake, Marni used to say it was in our blood.

In summer the lake glimmers, its surface reflecting sky, little clouds on little waves. It's the start of July now, and the lake is wide and green, like Mom's eyes. Sailboats are moored at the marina, and our yard tumbles down into the water, where our own small dock reaches in. Ours has just a canoe, ruby red. Dad named it *3 Grrrls*, for us: Mom, Marni, and me.

The lake is always changing. In autumn it's golden,

floating leaves of red and yellow stretching like fingers across its shores. This is where the geese gather, deciding who will lead south the first frosty morning. Marni and I used to crouch in the cattails and wave goodbye each fall. When winter comes, the lake is a white stretch of icing atop a giant wedding cake. The skaters glide across it like little figurines, making swirls in the frosting. The lake is where I laced up my first pair of Christmas skates, white as snow. And where I fell hard, so hard that it knocked the wind out of me and Dad came running and Mom murmured, "It's all right, let your breath find you."

When the days get longer, our lake shifts and creaks. Dad says the ice is talking. Soon it melts, and come spring there is that smell, an earthy scent that surfaces from murky depths, deep, deep down. The lake comes back to life, the ducks return, and buds burst green and red. When I open my window on April days, I can smell it, green and lush and thick. But since it's summer, there's more for one's senses. In addition to smelling it, I hear it. I hear the splashing swimmers, the purring motors of boats. The lifeguard's whistle at the private beach around the bend. And this year I also hear a silence, one that fills me with a sense of darkness and cold. Like how I imagine the bottom of the lake is in winter. I do not swim there anymore. It is different now, not just in season but different from any summer before. This summer Mom and Marni have left us with this lake. And I draw my curtains closed, so I won't see it.

The Family

My full name is Amelia Wallace Martin, but everyone calls me Lace. Wallace was my grandmother's last name. Somehow it got shortened, and now it's me. You might think since I'm named after Grandma Wallace we are real close, or alike in some way. I can assure you, we are neither. That name is the only thing Grandma Wallace and I share. Grandma Wallace is my mom's mother, and she is from what we call the proper side of the family. Holidays spent at the Wallaces' are stiff. There is a lot of sitting up straight, whether it's around the Christmas tree or at a table for someone's birthday cake. They don't like dogs, not even Cinder, and everyone likes Cinder. The Wallaces take small bites of their food, and speak in whispers when something shocking is discussed. And a lot appears to shock them. Like the time I ran around the lake in my diaper. Never mind that I was a tiny baby at a beach picnic. Diapers were not meant to be seen, and baby girls were not meant to run like wild animals, half naked. That, according to Grandma Wallace, was shocking.

The Martins, Dad's side of the family, don't shock much at all. In fact, Grampa Martin himself had forgotten his swim trunks the day of that picnic, and it was a scorching hot one. According to Dad, Grampa just pulled off all his clothes, right down to his plaid boxer shorts, in front of everyone. Then he did a cannonball into the lake, hooting and hollering and splashing around. I wish someone had taken a photo of Grandma Wallace's face at that moment. *That* must've been shocking.

When Marni and Mom left for Portland two weeks ago, the only true shock I have ever experienced, I did not get to see if the Wallaces pinched their lips or whispered behind their hands. In fact, the Wallaces didn't come. But the Martins couldn't stop. Gran and Grampa, who I call the Grands, drove the three hours from their home in Vermont, and my aunt and uncle flew in from California. There were Gran and Grampa Martin sleeping on the pull-out sofa in the downstairs den, Uncle Matt and his kids squeezed into the guest room. And there was Aunt Mae, Dad's younger sister, sleeping on a cot by my bed, her long dark hair spilling over the pillow, so close I could reach out and touch it. No one asked to stay in Marni's room. Each night Aunt Mae sat up and whispered to me in the dark, until my eyelids fluttered with sleep. She didn't tell me it was going to be all right, and she didn't say that Marni and Mom would be home soon. Instead we talked about Cinder, or about school, things you might expect to talk about if everything was normal. I loved Aunt Mae for talking to me like that, most of all for the things we didn't talk about.

When Mom and Marni went away, Dad went with them. At first. He came home about a week later, alone. Now he'll go back and forth each week, driving the hours south. The Martins will keep me company when Dad leaves. And Mom calls us every night to check in with us. But nothing is the same. When Mom and Marni left, our sense of order left with them. When the Martins aren't here to help, the kitchen sink is always full of dishes, and the laundry spills out the dryer, around the corner of the mudroom like a cotton snake coiling its way to the bedrooms. Dad has tried to keep up; he even stopped work for a while. Gran and Grampa invited me to stay with them for the summer. But I couldn't leave Dad alone. So for a couple weeks we all camped out in the house, cramped together, eating and sleeping like a family does, and we kept at it until everyone got tired. By the end of June, Gran's and Grampa's backs grew tired of the pullout couch, and Dad got tired of tripping over suitcases. I got tired of pretending everything was all right.

"It's time we all get back to normal," Grampa Martin said. Dad nodded, as though this was something we could easily do. We put on our bravest faces and waved goodbye. I felt a relief come over me when Grampa's red truck rattled out of the driveway, returning them to their own home. But mine felt emptier than ever.

Pancakes

"She's up!" Dad ruffles my ponytail as I plop myself at the kitchen table. "Pancakes for my girl?" he asks. Cinder scoots under the table and licks my toe. The stove gurbles and glugs, noises that do not sound like pancake frying to me.

"Really, Dad, I can just have cereal. It's fine."

"No, no. Mom always makes strawberry pancakes in summer. So will we. Now, does it usually bubble like this?" He drops the spatula, and gooey paste splatters the cupboard door. Behind him the griddle smokes, more of the same paste oozing over the sides onto the burner.

"I think we have a situation," he yells, whisking the pan from the stove. It's the first thing Dad always says whenever anything goes wrong. And this breakfast looks really wrong.

"I think Mom usually mixes all that stuff in a bowl first."

"Oh," Dad says, and sighs. He gives the blob a poke with a finger, then dumps the whole thing in the sink.

"Cereal it is," I say.

I open my sketchbook to my latest drawing. It's of Cinder's face, sort of a portrait. I grab a red pencil to color in the lobsters that dance across his dog collar. Every summer Mom gets us new swimsuits, and Cinder gets a new collar. Not this year. So I scrubbed his old collar real good. The red lobsters have faded a little, but it looks almost new. It's navy blue with a big brass buckle. When I'm satisfied with the lobsters, I grab my storm gray pencil and work on his ears. The left one's a little too pointy.

"So what's the plan today?" Dad's voice is too cheerful, and he looks at me with too much hope. It makes me want to hug him. He's just returned from Portland, without the rest of my family, but with a deep furrow in his brow that twitches each time he looks at me. I turn back to my sketchbook.

Summer was something I had looked forward to. Endless days of swimming and ice creams at the Snack Shack under the hot sun. But that all changed on June 16, just two weeks ago. The Saturday that destroyed everything. Now, July stretches before me like a path into a dark forest. I look at Dad and shrug apologetically. I don't have any big plans. I don't want any.

"Not much," I tell him. And then I add quickly, "Maybe I'll go to the pool with Beth Ann."

Dad looks relieved. "What a great idea! Here's some money for cheeseburgers." This makes him happy, so I take the five dollars he offers and stuff it in my pocket.

The Corner of Pratt

Beth Ann Watts is waiting for me on the corner of Pratt Street. Beth Ann is not what you would call popular, but she is certainly well known. We met in nursery school. She stood out to me right away because she was the only kid who didn't have a blankey. What she did have was a handkerchief. A monogrammed, yellow hankie that went everywhere she went. But don't be fooled by thinking that maybe it was a blankey substitute, 'cause Beth Ann never was a thumb sucker. That habit was dirty. Dirty habits were everywhere. So were dirty surfaces. That little yellow hankie was for cleaning all things in our preschool classroom: a door handle, a purple crayon, and Whinny, the rocking horse. She was quick with that hankie, even as a four-year-old. You could say, "Hey, Beth Ann, let's play dolls." And before you could kneel by the dolly crib she'd have all those dolls lined up on the floor, stripped right down to their plastic nakedness, wiping every hand and foot and head with that hankie. "Okay," she'd assure me, dusting off that hankie, "you can touch them now." Beth Ann doesn't carry that hankie anymore. These days she carries a little pack of disinfectant wipes. I can always tell if Beth Ann is in school before me, because I'll detect a faint scent of Clorox in the classroom doorway. But despite her war on germs, Beth Ann has always been my best friend. Really, she is the one friend I have.

Since Marni and Mom left, everyone acts too careful around me, like I'm suddenly breakable or something. Beth Ann never does that. And she doesn't ask why I wear my clothes to the pool, why my swimsuit stays zipped in my backpack, wrapped neatly in a towel that will not get wet. Instead she waits at the corner of Pratt Street with her big glasses all crooked on her small face, her hair in two babyish pigtails even though we are thirteen years old now, the skirt of her neon green bathing suit stuck in the spokes of her bike tire. She almost tips over when I ride up next to her.

"You okay?" I ask as I steady her handlebars.

"Yes, yes," she assures me, adjusting her glasses. "I'm just trying out my new bike. Dad put wide tires on it for better traction. He's experimenting." Beth Ann's father is an inventor, and he is always messing with things that work just fine the way they are. As she pedals down the sidewalk, she teeters dangerously close, swerves off the curb, and bounces back on.

"Maybe we should slow down?" she worries.

"Beth Ann, if we go any slower we'll stop." It's true. Her baby brother could crawl faster than we're going. "Maybe if we go faster you'll get your balance?"

"No, no, that would be dangerous." I am used to this, and although I disagree, I do not say so. Instead I keep a safe distance and practice the face I'll make at the pool. Happy, but not too happy. Maybe a little distracted, like I'm having too much fun to notice anyone. Serious, like I'm reading a good book. Then nobody will bug me. Next time I'll have to remember to bring a big book.

Pratt Pool was Marni's favorite summer hangout, besides the lake. This past year she'd made the high school varsity swim team, the Saybrook Trout. She was the only sophomore on the team, and being a Trout was her life. She held the records for both the 200- and 100-meter women's freestyle, with times of 1:53.99 and 57:55 respectively. She was their golden girl. Wherever she went she wore some part of the team: the team jacket, the T-shirt, or the baseball hat. The *S.T.* initials were even drawn on her backpack. During summer she swam on the town team, dubbed the Summer Trout. They held lessons and practiced at Pratt Pool, but they competed in the open water of the lake. *The real deal,* Marni liked to say, trotting down to the water's edge and pulling her cap over her hair.

Swimming was her life. When Marni wasn't in the water, she was doing dry-land exercises. Stretching, weight training, jumping rope. Always focused on being stronger, faster. I loved to swim, too, but it wasn't like that for me. It's no stretch of the truth to say that everyone who knows

Marni Martin loves her, and everyone who meets Lace Martin gets that look. It's the look people get when they see the sequel to a really good movie but it leaves them wanting. Like the second part just doesn't live up to the first. Of course, I never said this to Marni. She'd tell me the wind was blowing in one ear and out the other. Marni never tried to be the best, it just wasn't in her. But I think she knew. While our report cards are all A's, Marni's have pluses next to them. And when we both ace the swim test each summer, it's Marni with the fastest times in all four strokes, even beating the boys. And when the swim test's over, it's Marni the boys plop themselves next to on the dock. Especially the ones she beat.

The Question

"What flavor?" It's my favorite question. Since Beth Ann is a bit of a health nut, I'd had to convince her to join me in a cone.

"Vanilla!" we both yell at once.

"Is this ice cream organic?" Beth Ann asks the kid behind the counter as he hands us our cones.

"Organic?"

"Yes, *organic*. As in no pesticides, no preservatives, no chemicals used in the making of this food product?"

He stares at us blankly.

"I prefer organic," she tells him matter-of-factly. "You should, too."

I steer her away from the counter. "It's ice cream, Beth Ann. Just eat it."

The pool is alive, kids bobbing up down, up down. Mothers recline on beach chairs. Beth Ann and I plop down beside each other on an empty chair and work on our cones.

"Must you do that?" I groan.

Beth Ann's cone is covered in fresh white napkins— from home, since any public napkin is surely contaminated. She's wrapped her cone so severely you can't see what flavor it is. She has to lick down into it, her tongue disappearing deep into the napkin layers. She ignores my question.

"Can you even taste it?" I ask.

"Hello, Lace," a voice says.

I shade my eyes and look up. It's too bright to see who's there, but the snooty tone is familiar. Jade Winslow sits herself on a lounge chair next to us with a bounce. She stretches her legs out and starts applying sunscreen in long, slow strokes, carefully adjusting her jewelry. "You poor thing." She reaches over to pat my knee like I am a child.

Jade Winslow is in high school. She's never talked to me, even though she's in Marni's class. And she's never invited either of us to her annual start-of-summer party.

I know why she's sitting here now. I concentrate on my cone.

"Any news from Portland?"

I feel Beth Ann stiffen beside me, but she doesn't say anything. I shake my head and lick faster.

It doesn't stop Jade. "I haven't seen you at the lake. Not doing Summer Trout this year?"

"No." I have not been in the lake since that day. It's been weird enough coming to the pool and not seeing Marni with her teammates.

"You must miss your mom." She pauses. "And Marni, of course. My mother says she may never come back. Is that true?" Jade Winslow stares at me.

My heart is pounding so hard now I can't answer. The pool blurs. Suddenly Beth Ann comes to life beside me.

"I forgot!" she yells. She hops up, flipping the beach chair over, and we both slide off onto the grass. "We have to go! I forgot about my piano lesson!" She trips over her towel, flailing like a fish. Her glasses land in a bush, and she crawls around snatching at the grass.

Jade Winslow laughs, but I don't care. I reach for Beth Ann and help unravel the beach towel from her skinny legs. We run to the pool gate.

"Do you really have piano?" I ask Beth Ann.

She's puffing hard, wiping grass from her glasses. "Well, sure I do. On Thursday."

Today is Tuesday, and I squeeze her hand.

The Closed Door

Marni's bedroom door has been closed for two weeks now, and I almost expect it to creak when I enter, but it doesn't, of course. Inside, her striped curtains hang still against the closed windows and a loose pile of competitive swim magazines wait beside the bed like she just dropped them there. The bedcovers are tossed back and rumpled, as if she hopped out of them only this morning. I run my fingers over her favorite jeans, the ones with the hole in the right knee, thrown over her chair. It's like she could walk back in any minute and pull them on before running down to the beach to see her friends. Her swim tanks hang quietly on the closet door, giving the room the faintest scent of chlorine.

Dad and I never talk about Marni's room. On days when all the floors get vacuumed or the beds get made, this room is left undisturbed. The door simply stays shut, like there isn't anything on the other side.

Already it's a sort of museum. There are some things I touch, real careful, so I don't move them. For some reason it's become important that everything stays right where she left it. Like last season's swim trophies, lined boldly on her dresser, four in all. And the photos on her bulletin board. Last year's school notebooks rest on her desk. When I flip through, the margins of every page are covered with smiley faces, notes from friends, and the letters *S.T.*, Saybrook Trout, her life. The last thing I touch on my way out is her silver hairbrush. From it drape long shiny brown strands, and if I press it to my nose, it smells like sun and sand and grass. Like her. I worry someday it won't anymore.

Marni never liked me going through her stuff without permission, and so I don't. I wander around, sometimes touching a few things, and then I leave it as she did. Before, Marni would've chucked a royal fit if she found me in her room, although that never stopped me. Now I can come in here anytime I want, and yet I don't. It's funny how you don't listen to a person when they're right there with you, when you should be listening. And suddenly, when they aren't around, you start hearing what they said. I try to look at people when they talk to me now. I want them to know that I hear them, that I'm listening hard to what they say, and that it does matter.

Mrs. Dodge

We need help. The laundry has finally been done, but the baskets still line the mudroom floor waiting to be put away and the unopened mail teeters precariously in a growing mountain on the counter. Cinder hasn't had a bath since the beginning of June.

"We've got to do something about this dog," Dad says, pinching his nose.

"But he only lets Mom do it," I protest.

"He stinks, Lace. He needs a bath."

Cinder grins, and I hand him a piece of toast. "I think he likes his stink."

"That may be, but I don't. It's bath day today or he stays outside."

In the backyard I fill our old kiddie pool with water. There were only five biscuits left in the jar. Cinder eyes me as I pull one from my pocket.

"Here, boy." I lure him down the steps, across the yard, and up to the pool. I've almost got him. "Just one more step!" The hose spurts behind me. Cinder halts, his whiskered nose snuffling the air. I try to kick the shampoo bottle behind the pool, but it's too late. He knows. I lunge for his collar.

"You'll like this," I gasp as he drags me across the wet grass. It takes all my strength to wrestle him back to the kiddie pool. "Welcome to the beauty parlor," I huff, heaving him over the side and into the water. Cinder turns and glares at me.

"So, Mr. Stinky, will we be doing a new hairstyle today, or just a rinse?" He growls quietly and sinks into the pool. "Good choice," I tell him. I try to remember how Mom does it.

First I soak him from shoulder to tail. Once he's good and wet, I start working him over with the soap. He doesn't seem to mind this part, and even jigs his hind leg happily when I scrub a good spot on his belly. "Just think how spiffy you'll look." Cinder frowns at me from under a crown of bubbles. His whole black body is white with foam.

"All right, Mr. Stinky. Time for your complimentary rinse." Just as I reach for the bucket, the neighbor's tabby cat streaks from the bushes. Mr. Stinky comes to life. The whole pool rocks, and my knees buckle as I slide into the sudsy water.

"Cinder, stop!" But he is out of the pool, a wiggly, wet noodle of a dog, homing in on the tail of Mrs. Pringle's cat.

By the time I catch up, Cinder is wriggling up the porch steps. I chase him through the kitchen, where we both zigzag by the bags of groceries waiting to be unpacked. He screeches to a halt at the stove, licking the remnants of Dad's breakfast from the floor. The pancake griddle's still in the sink, and the phone rings from under a dish towel. I answer it.

"Lacey Bean! How's my girl?" Gran's voice ripples through the room like she's here.

"Fine," I tell her as my eyes roam from Cinder to the overflowing sink.

"I'm glad to hear that, darling. Any word from your mother?" I suck in my breath.

"Nothing new, Gran."

She sighs, and the other end of the phone goes quiet. I imagine all her ruby rings clanking together as she wrings her hands. Suddenly I want to get off the phone.

"Well, darling, you let us know if you need anything. You and your dad doing anything special for the Fourth?" The Fourth of July. I glance at the calendar on the wall. Apparently, Dad had forgotten, just like me.

"Sure, Gran," I lie. "Hot dogs, hamburgers, the works." No need for her to worry.

"Oh good," she says. "And remember, if you hear anything, anything at all, you'll let us know?"

"I will," I promise.

Cinder scampers around me in soapy circles as I put the receiver back.

"Dad?" I call out. There's no answer. Mom doesn't like when we shout across the house for each other. Remembering this, I take the stairs two at a time, hopping over the same old baskets of laundry that Dad must have started to bring up and forgot about.

"In my office, Lace. Just working on a project."

Dad's "office" is a little desk tucked into the corner of my parents' bedroom. Dad is an architect, and he used to go into his real office, in town, regularly. But just last week he came home with piles of folders and set up an office upstairs. He says it has nothing to do with me. He says it's quiet and he likes working at the tiny makeshift desk Grampa Martin made for him. But we both know different.

Cinder sneaks up the stairs and slips down the hall, a line of muddy prints trailing his wagging behind. I block the door.

"Was that Cinder? You're done with the dog bath already?"

I shrug. "Yeah, um, it looks that way. Want me to put away the groceries next?"

Dad slouches, twisting the pencil behind his ear. "Oh yeah. The groceries." The furrow in his brow twitches once, then again.

"I've got it, Dad," I tell him. I decide not to mention that it's the Fourth of July.

Behind us someone sneezes, and we both turn. In the doorway drips Cinder. There are soapsuds in the matted fur on his chest and bubbles atop his muzzle. A wide puddle pools on the floor beneath his wet tummy. He sneezes again, and squeezes through my legs into the bedroom.

"Oh no . . ." breathes Dad, diving protectively atop the stack of papers on his desk.

But before I can catch him, Cinder winds up, shaking left then right, a storm of suds spraying the walls of the room. I turn to Dad, who stands up and calmly wipes dog hair from his glasses. He sighs and sets his pencil on his wet desk.

"Lace, I'm afraid we have a situation."

I brace myself.

"We can't keep this up by ourselves. And we can't expect Gran and Grampa to keep going back and forth."

"But we're not by ourselves! Mom'll be back in a few weeks," I protest.

Dad shakes his head. "Lace, we don't really know if that's true."

"She will, Dad. She promised!" I can feel the tears in my eyes.

"Lace, it's taken care of." He reaches for a small blue brochure that's folded on his desk and slides it to me like a secret note.

"This is the agency the hospital recommended. They offer all kinds of services: domestic help, caregivers, people who know how to help families with . . . a situation like ours." He pauses and clears his throat. "I hired someone yesterday, and she starts tomorrow."

"Tomorrow?"

Dad wipes a stray soap bubble from his nose and raises his eyebrows. I can tell he wants me to like this idea. But I don't. I don't like the thought of someone else in our house. Some stranger doing our laundry or bathing Cinder. Mom would do that when she came home. She would take care of us, make us laugh, cook our dinners.

"And thank goodness, she cooks, too," Dad says, and smiles. "Her name is Willa Dodge."

The Green Suitcase

The next day Willa Dodge heaves herself through the front door. It's not that she is short, though she is. Or a bit on the fat side, though she's that, too. What's really weighing her down is a reptile green suitcase hoisted across her chest. It's full to bursting. She waddles in, her stocky arms wrapped tightly about it. I cover my mouth and try not to laugh. It looks like she's wrestling a giant crocodile.

"You must be Willa. Good morning!" My father hurries out from under the sink to help her. His button-down shirt is all wet, and he drops the wrench and wipes his hand before shaking hers. Willa Dodge nods, pulls a black duffel bag off her shoulder, and shoves it into his outreached arms. She does not surrender the green suitcase. Nor does she say hello.

"Willa, this is Lace."

She nods at me over her suitcase and waddles past like she knows where she's going. Dad hurries behind her, still trying to relieve her of the green bag.

"Uh, Willa, can I . . ." Willa Dodge has a grip on the green suitcase like a steel trap, and she continues through the kitchen, dragging Dad behind like an old sack. By the time she's trudged into the living room, he's given up.

"Well, let's show you to your room. It's just . . ." He points upstairs, but before Dad can direct her further, Willa Dodge is already puffing up the stairs. Dad's jaw drops open, but no sound comes out. I shrug.

"Uh, just make yourself at home," he calls after her disappearing figure. We listen as she makes her way down the hall, and eventually the guest room door slaps shut.

"Jeez," I mutter, but Dad's already back to fidgeting under the sink.

"Oh, dear."

"Dad?"

There is a clink, followed by a gush. Dad's legs jolt, and his wrench flies out on a geyser of water.

"I think we have a situation," he yells.

The Keeper

There is a note in my dresser drawer that has been unfolded so many times in the past few weeks that already the creases are like flannel. It's a short note to Mom and Dad, scrawled quickly in blue pen. The paper isn't fancy stationery with flowers or anything; in fact, it's not stationery at all. The note's written on the back of a used envelope. It doesn't say much; like I said, it's short. And it doesn't even have my name on it, so it's not like it was addressed to me. But the contents aren't private. It says this:

Hey, Mom and Dad,

> *Gone down to the lake with S.T. Back for dinner. Cinder's in the yard.*

> *xoxo M*

Like I said, it's a short note. It tells us that she went to the lake with the Saybrook Trout. And that she left Cinder at home. Thank God she did. I know he would've tried to help if he'd been with her. Maybe that's selfish, but he's all I've got this summer. Him and this note that was left on the kitchen table. This note that I found after we got the news, that I tucked into my pocket while Mom cried out loud, and quietly walked away with while Dad ran from the house. That I folded carefully into my sock drawer. It was not written to me, but I am the keeper of this note, the last words Marni left with us.

Organic

"Too skinny. You need to eat." Willa Dodge thunks a large piece of corn bread on Beth Ann's dinner plate later that night. We all jump.

"You, too!" She shakes a spoon at Dad. "Eat up!" We examine the table. A large bowl of beef stew, corn bread, and tomato salad for our first dinner together. It smells wonderful.

Cinder shimmies up beside Willa Dodge and grins. She frowns back.

"Shall I set a place for him?" The whole table rattles as Cinder wags his tail at this suggestion.

Dad laughs nervously. "Now, Cinder," he warns. The tail disappears under the table.

"Willa, this is great. Really great!" Dad beams at her across the table, a little trickle of stew on his chin as proof.

Willa Dodge clucks her tongue. "I think you have a situation on your chin." She thrusts a napkin in his direction.

Dad's right. We haven't eaten this well since Gran left last weekend. The bread is thick and heavy, soaking up the rich stew.

"Great tomatoes, Willa," Dad almost cheers.

I frown at him. *I'd* made the tomato salad that afternoon. Willa Dodge had only helped.

It started earlier that day, when I grabbed Cinder's leash and called him outside for a walk. I assumed Willa Dodge was still upstairs in her room, as we hadn't seen her since her arrival that morning. I was humming a little, Cinder's tail was wagging as he tugged on the leash in my hands, and we were just passing the garden gate when a giant head popped up over the fence.

"Disgraceful!" it said.

I screamed.

Cinder ducked behind me.

The head disappeared.

"Mrs. Dodge?" I whispered.

"Get a move on, chicken legs! I could use some help in here."

I dropped the leash and peeked over the gate. There, stooped among the beans and squash, her big aproned bottom looming above the eggplant, was Willa Dodge. Our garden was a mess, overgrown and weedy, the early tomatoes choking in the swirl of growth, like red balloons tangled in jungle branches.

"Are you gonna stand there gawking, or are ya gonna make yourself useful?"

Before I could answer, she'd tossed a pair of gardening gloves at my feet. I wasn't sure what to make of this, but Cinder appeared to know what to do. He'd curled up under the elm tree, one eye on his navy blue leash in case I tried to walk it without him.

We filled a basket with weeds, and another with the tomatoes we could rescue. I watched as Willa Dodge carefully clipped some lavender.

"That's my mom's," I told her, reaching suddenly for the bunch in her hand.

Willa Dodge relinquished the purple-tipped stems. I brought some to my nose and breathed deeply. It made my chest ache. "It's her favorite," I said more gently.

Willa Dodge nodded and passed me a bucket. "Why don't you fill this with lake water? It's good for the garden, makes the beans sing."

I eyed the bucket and swallowed hard, tucking the lavender into a basket by the gate.

"I'll just fill it from the faucet. It's closer."

Willa Dodge raised her eyebrows. "Lake water's better, but suit yourself."

I felt her eyes on my back as I trudged to the spigot and untangled the hose.

"Look out!" a familiar girl's voice hollered from up the road.

We both heard Beth Ann's arrival before we actually saw her. It started a few houses up, with a gentle rattle followed by a crash.

"Ouch!" yelled a man's voice.

"Sorry, so sorry," the girl shouted in reply.

As the rattling drew closer Willa Dodge pulled herself up, and I leaned over the fence. There, swerving left and right down our sidewalk, was Beth Ann. She veered suddenly left and plowed through the neighbor's shrubs before turning quickly back onto the sidewalk, a look of surprise on her face.

Beth Ann was never good on a bike, but something else was different. Then I saw the tires. There were double tires on the front and back of the bike—big, fat, bright purple tires. Like a grape moon buggy. Her father was at it again. Stuck in the spokes were leaves and branches and a few of Mrs. Pringle's roses, though I don't think Beth Ann's father had anything to do with those.

"Have mercy," breathed Willa Dodge.

Beth Ann rattled up in front of our house and jerked to a halt.

"My rosebushes!" cried Mrs. Pringle, who was now crouching over her shrubs next door.

"Sorry, Mrs. Pringle!" Beth Ann called. She struggled with her bike helmet as Willa Dodge sucked in her breath. "What do you think? Dad rigged up a four-wheeler!"

"You know this girl?" Willa asked.

"Mrs. Dodge, meet Beth Ann Watts."

Beth Ann grinned and stuck out her hand, disinfecting it quickly afterward. Willa Dodge didn't notice. She was leaning back like it was all too much.

"Wanna stay for dinner? We're having salad," I said.

"I guess," Beth Ann said, and shrugged. "But is your produce organic? I only eat organic. You know how I feel about vegetable pesticides."

I looked to see if Willa Dodge had heard, and she was scowling.

"Child, if you want organic, then you get down on those freckled knees and start picking." With that she tossed her gloves to Beth Ann, who held them at arm's length, inspecting them suspiciously. There was no time to disinfect. Willa Dodge was thrashing the eggplant mercilessly, and Beth Ann's eyes popped as she watched.

"Just put them on, Beth Ann," I pleaded, reaching for the watering can. "Just put them on."

Night Noises

On the first night of Willa Dodge, a strange noise wakes me up. My clock says it's after midnight. Was I dreaming? But then I hear it again. Footsteps coming up the stairs. Is it Dad? The top step creaks, and the footsteps grow louder. *Squeak, squeak, squeak.* They come closer, moving slowly toward my room, and I pull my covers up higher. Just outside my door the footsteps pause. The good news is that I hear Dad snoring on the other side of the wall, not far away. The bad news is that the footsteps are not his. Is it Willa Dodge?

The footsteps move on, past my door. Cinder stirs at the foot of my bed, and his eyes glow in the faint moonlight spilling through the window. I shiver and wait until the steps disappear down the hall before slipping carefully out of bed. The house is quiet, and the hall is empty when I peek out. Behind me Cinder rises and stretches.

"Come on," I whisper to him.

He wags his tail eagerly and rushes through the door,

as if to say, *Let's go!* In the hall he stops suddenly and sniffs the air. He whines, circling.

"What is it, boy?" I ask.

I watch as he trots down the hall and stops at Marni's door. He looks back at me, wagging his tail fiercely now.

"Marni's not in there," I tell him.

But Cinder doesn't buy it. He paws the door, scratching with his nails.

"Cinder, come!" I whisper firmly.

But he raises his nose, sniffing the air urgently. He's picked up a scent, something familiar.

"Where are you going?" I call as he races away.

Nose to the ground, he tracks the scent down the hall, whining loudly as he goes.

"Shhh," I warn.

As I follow, I feel the wet floor beneath my feet. And I, too, smell something in the air. It is oddly familiar, an earthy smell, like mud and rain. Cinder trots along the wet trail and halts outside Willa Dodge's door. There he sits, looking over his shoulder at me, smiling.

"What, Cinder? What is it?"

It's then I notice the footprints, damp and faint, leading right up to her door.

It's something Cinder recognizes. Something that makes him miss Marni. I follow him down the hall to Willa Dodge's door, tiptoeing quietly. When I'm almost there, I hear it. A loud, long *sssh* sound, almost a hiss. I press myself flat against the wall. It's not a voice but a familiar noise . . . a zipper. The sound of something big, like a sleeping bag. Then I know. It's the sound of the giant green suitcase being carefully zipped up.

The Wink

At breakfast I try to catch Dad's eye. I want to ask him if he heard the noises in the night, too. But his face is buried in the morning paper. Willa Dodge is bustling around the kitchen, clattering breakfast pans and pouring juice. I watch her closely for clues. Why had she been in the lake last night? And what was she up to? The hall floor was dry this morning, and the footprints had been mopped away.

Willa Dodge catches me staring at her, and she shoves more eggs on my plate. "Still hungry?"

"No, no thank you." Just in case Willa Dodge is dangerous, I smile up at her. You don't want to make a crazy person mad. So I show her my biggest smile, so big it makes my lips feel like taffy. She and Dad are both staring at me now.

"Lace, is something wrong with your mouth?" Dad asks.

At least I've got the man's attention. Willa Dodge

turns back to the sink, and I wink at him and nod toward the door.

Dad frowns. I wink again, and wag my head to the side.

"Do you have pool water in your ear or something?"

I give up and eat the stupid eggs.

"Did you know Willa gave Cinder a bath this morning?" Dad looks pleased.

"What? He let her?" I peer under the table. There, wagging his tail sheepishly, is the shiniest dog I've ever seen.

He yawns happily and shrugs, as if to say, *I'm sorry, but don't I look good?*

"Traitor," I whisper.

"Well, I've gotta run," Dad says, glancing quickly at his empty wrist. "What time is it anyway?" he asks, looking flustered.

"Nine o'clock, Mr. Martin," Willa Dodge answers.

"Can't find my watch," Dad tells me, as he stands to go.

"You lost it?" I ask. Dad has an engraved gold watch that Mom gave him for their first anniversary. He never leaves the house without it.

"I can't imagine what happened to it," he says, shaking his head. "I'm sure I put it on my bedside table last night, just like I always do."

"Mom will be upset. We've got to find it."

"I know, I know," Dad says sadly. "I've been looking all morning. It's like it just disappeared."

Willa Dodge eyes me over her shoulder from the sink, the green dish towel flashing in and out of the pot she's drying. For a minute I see the green suitcase, clutched to her chest like a dark secret.

Pool Gods and Orange Beetles

"Sully Tanner is a god," Beth Ann whispers.

I look up from my sketchbook. Spread in the grass beside me are my blue and green pastels: aqua, cobalt, meadow. The pool stretches across the paper like a puddle.

"What did you just say?" I ask, and laugh as Beth Ann's freckles burn crimson.

"Well, he is," she mumbles. I squint at the far end of the pool. Dad says people have their own opinions, but what Beth Ann said is closer to a truth. Sully Tanner balances on the edge of the diving board, his brown back to us. When he glances over his broad shoulder, his hair glistens with pool water.

"Oh my lord. Did he just smile at us?" Beth Ann gasps.

I'm pretty sure he didn't, but before I can say so Sully pushes off the board into a reverse flip. A chorus of cheers erupts, and Beth Ann sways on the blanket beside me. Even the mothers on beach chairs look up from their magazines. Sully surfaces, grinning widely. He is really something.

Beth Ann grabs my hand. "I signed up for swim lessons this summer. I've decided to go out for swim team in the fall."

"Because of Sully Tanner?" I ask, trying unsuccessfully to hide my surprise.

"No!" She looks hurt. "Because I want to."

I look at Beth Ann and I want to say something nice, but I can't think of anything. "But you don't really swim," I remind her, picturing her flailing dog paddle, which barely gets her from one side of the shallow end to the other.

She gives me a wounded look. "I do, too! I just need to practice my technique."

Beth Ann is not exactly what you'd call athletic. Last spring we joined the girls' softball team. All season Beth Ann dropped balls and struck out. In our last game, when she finally got her first hit, she ran the bases. Backward. We were all yelling at her, telling her, "Wrong way, go back," but she thought we were cheering her on and just ran faster. "At least she's quick," Dad had said.

Beth Ann is still frowning. "It's the beginner class," she says softly. "Not everyone's a natural like you. And Marni."

I look at her face now, and I know she's waiting for me to say something. I think of what Beth Ann just said, especially about Marni. She was the best of them all. And she knows that Beth Ann can barely dog-paddle. But if she were here now, she wouldn't tell Beth Ann she's crazy. She'd say something nice. So I put down my pastels and look Beth Ann real hard in the eye and say it.

"Marni would be proud of you."

Her whole face lights up.

"Excuse me, Lace?" someone interrupts. We look up into the endless blue that is Sully Tanner's eyes.

I cannot speak. Beth Ann's elbow jolts me.

"Lace!" she whispers.

"Yeah, I'm Lace," I stammer.

His grin is wider. "I know."

I cannot believe Sully Tanner knows my first name.

"So, how are things?" he asks, stepping back and shaking his blond head dry like a dog.

Beth Ann leans into its spray, practically melting.

"Okay," I tell him.

Beth Ann thrusts her freckled arm under his nose.

"I'm Beth Ann Watts. I'm taking beginner swim," she gushes.

Sully smiles politely. "Is that so?" He turns back to me. "How 'bout you, Lace? I noticed you weren't on the team."

"No. Not this summer," I mumble.

Sully looks away and nods thoughtfully.

"Right," he says. "I understand. Well, don't be a stranger." He smiles once more, in my direction, before turning to go. "Oh yeah, and I guess I'll see you for lessons, Betty." He gives her a thumbs-up.

Beth Ann perks up and then slumps back down. "It's Beth Ann," she mumbles, but Sully Tanner is already walking away.

"He knows me," I say, barely breathing.

"I know," Beth Ann says with a sigh. "I bet he knows everyone. Except me."

"Don't worry," I assure her, picking up my sketchbook. "He'll know you if you take swim lessons."

She nods, a smile creeping back on her face. "So, what'd you think of Willa Dodge?" I ask, switching the subject. I turn to a new page in my sketchbook and reach for a charcoal pencil.

"She's a good cook," Beth Ann says.

"Not as good as Mom," I tell her. I draw a plump, dark figure with a large pumpkin head. On top I swirl the charcoal around and around, until an alarming smokestack of curls erupts from her head.

"And besides, she's a thief."

"A thief?" Beth Ann looks at me with surprise.

"Yeah, I think she stole my dad's gold watch." I pencil in two black, beady eyes.

"Are you sure it's not just missing? My dad loses stuff all the time." She's rummaging through her beach bag for her big, ugly green goggles. I'm hoping she left them home.

"No, Dad would never misplace it. Someone must

have taken it, and that someone is her." I look at the round face in my sketchbook and draw two fangs protruding from the lips. "I think she's a weirdo."

Beth Ann peers over at my picture. "You're the weirdo," she says, poking me with her big toe. Her nails are painted bright orange. They're the same color as this old Volkswagen Beetle we used to have.

Marni loved that car. Sometimes when we were little, we'd dress up and pretend to be old ladies out on a Sunday drive: Mabel and Gladys. She'd wear this wide-brimmed pink straw hat and drape herself in one of Mom's fancy shawls. If Marni was quick, she'd get the blond wig we'd found at a tag sale that we always fought over. My favorite item was a lobster red boa from the back of Mom's closet. Then we'd load our necks with pearls until we could barely stagger out the door in our high heels.

"We have to look elegant, like those city people," Marni would say in a fake British accent. Neither of us actually knew anyone from the city, let alone anyone with a British accent, but it somehow completed the idea.

I remember one afternoon we'd climbed into the orange VW Beetle, Marni behind the wheel. Our neighbor Mrs. Pringle sneered over the fence into our driveway. "A vehicle is not a toy!" she hissed. "Does your father know you're out here?"

I pretended not to hear, but Marni honked the horn.

"Out of the way, Mrs. Pringle, or we may run you over!" Marni was brave.

"Look at that fancy restaurant," I said, pointing out the window.

"Yes, Mabel, but let's not eat there this time. Terrible food, remember? The fish gave you gas!"

"Yes, and their soup had worms!" I added.

"Gassy fish and wormy soup?" she exclaimed. "The nerve!" And we rolled back and forth hysterically on the front seat as Marni pretended to swerve the car.

"Are you girls still playing in that car?" Mrs. Pringle yelled through the rosebushes.

"Darling, watch out for that cow!" I cried, pointing.

"Mabel, that was no cow. That was Mrs. Pringle!" And then we shrieked some more.

Dad took a picture of us in that car, wearing big sunglasses and old-lady outfits. "You two are about the hippest old ladies I ever saw," he said, laughing.

"But of course, dahling," Marni responded with a giggle.

That afternoon was a long time ago. Beth Ann wiggles her painted toes and stands up. "Want to go for a swim?" she asks hopefully.

I shake my head. "Maybe later," I say, swiping at a stray tear and reaching for my orange pastel.

Long Distance

When the phone rings at night, it's usually her. Dad cradles the receiver gently against his shoulder and paces, a look of grave focus in his eyes, the little furrow twitching methodically between his brows. It starts with a long silence as he listens to her update, nodding thoughtfully as if they were in the same room, separated by a mere coffee table instead of miles. Periodically he'll ask questions, in a slow, clinical tone, trying hard to keep the emotion from creeping in. Eventually his face relaxes a little, the brow smoothed by her voice or by the brief contact with a wife he misses and the news she has to offer. But usually the sad plains of his face sag, tired with the effort of listening, the strain of worrying about things he cannot fix pulling the corners of his mouth slack with exhaustion.

It is at this time that I tiptoe out after my period of quiet hovering. I've heard what I needed, deciphered what was necessary. And that is enough. I take my quiet leave before I can be summoned and the phone passed. The funny thing is I want to hear her voice. Desperately. I want to feel she is closer than the many miles we both know separate us. I just don't want to ask any questions, to force her to sugarcoat things in a way I know she will. Ultimately, though, it's the answers she cannot give that scare me the most.

But tonight Dad finds me in the doorway, touches my shoulder, then squeezes it gently. And so this night I take the phone.

"Hi, Mom," I whisper.

"I miss you, baby," she whispers back.

I close my eyes. I smell lavender.

Night Noises II

I set my flashlight by my pillow and scoot under my covers. Tonight I will follow Willa Dodge. And find Dad's watch. I lie awake for what seems like hours, listening as Dad closes the house up downstairs and eventually climbs the steps to his room next door. I wait while Cinder snores quietly at the foot of my bed. And just as my own eyes grow heavy, I hear a noise. A door shuts down the hall. And then there are footsteps, steps that move right past my door and continue down the stairs, the bottom step squeaking in the dark like a warning signal.

Whatever Willa Dodge is doing up at night doesn't make sense. Is she stealing from us? And hiding the loot outside? That must be it, I decide. She's looting the house in the middle of the night and hiding our stuff down by the lake. Stuff like Dad's watch.

When the house is quiet again, I peer carefully into the hall. Cinder streaks past me, racing down the stairs.

"Cinder!" I whisper loudly, but he is gone. When I peer over the landing below, the living room is empty. I hurry downstairs. I can always claim I'm letting Cinder out, and then I can catch Willa Dodge red-handed and call Dad. But there is no one downstairs when I get there, not even Cinder. I walk into the kitchen, where the screen door slaps quietly in the breeze. They must be outside.

The porch is damp and dewy underfoot, the air balmy but cool. I look into the backyard and see Cinder's tail zigging and zagging across the yard as he tracks something through the grass. Probably some poor opossum. I wrap my bathrobe more tightly around me and stare out into the darkness. It's then I see a pale figure in the distance, making her way through the trees. Toward the lake. I shiver. Even though this is my house and my yard, I'm hesitant to follow. I get halfway down the porch stairs and stop, straining to catch sight of her again. The moon is half full, casting more shadows than light across our yard, and I can't see her anymore. My heart pounds as I move across the grass. I have every right to follow her. And she has no right to be out here at night, sneaking around our place. But with every step I take in her direction, my heart pounds harder.

It's not Willa Dodge that bothers me. The smell of the lake fills the night, piercing my lungs as I stand at the yard's edge. There is a watery shimmer ahead, the hemlock trees lined against it like black paper cutouts that someone has placed there while we sleep. A breeze rises off the water, rustles the leaves overhead, fills the sky with the sound of rushing water. I want to go on, I really do. But I can't.

The Missing Bag

"He put his arms around me! Sully Tanner put his arms around *me*." Beth Ann flops dramatically on my bed the next evening. Her red pigtails swing back and forth as she hugs my purple pillow. "You should've been there!"

"He *hugged* you?" I ask, unable to hide my disbelief.

"Well, kind of. He was assisting me with my floating technique at the pool today. My swim lessons start next week."

I want to say, *You mean he held you up so you didn't sink like a ton of bricks*, but I don't. Instead I picture Sully Tanner's strong arms and wonder what they would feel like if they hugged me. A tickle runs down my back.

"And then he said, 'See you Monday, Beth Ann.' Don't you think that means something?" Her eyes flutter.

"But don't you have swim lessons on Monday?" I ask.

"That's not the point, Lace." She huffs and rolls over.

Just then someone passes my open bedroom door.

Suddenly there is a crash and a bang from downstairs. "Not again!" I hear my father yell.

We hurry downstairs to find Dad squished under the kitchen sink, a spray of water shooting through the cabinet doors. It winds across the kitchen and under the table, a little river on our hardwood floor.

"Dad," I say, as Beth Ann and I negotiate the watery mess, "you've got to call a plumber!"

"No, no, it's just a little drip," he assures me, and there is a clink followed by a clatter. The gush surges, and Beth Ann and I duck.

Willa Dodge enters the kitchen behind us and peers at Dad under the sink, her hands on her hips. "Mr. Martin, I'd be happy to help with that," she says.

Dad peeks out at us. "Oh, that's not necessary, thank you. It's under control now." As soon as he says it, the spray surges and we jump back.

"Sir, really," Willa Dodge persists, grabbing a hand towel from the rack.

I'm about to look for the phone book when the spray suddenly stops. "Got it!" yells my father victoriously.

We towel ourselves off as he emerges from under the sink, a wide grin plastered across his face. "Just needed a little elbow grease," he tells us proudly.

Willa Dodge rolls her eyes. "Right," she says. "Well, I'm off for an evening stroll." And with that she is out the screen door.

"I'd better get home," Beth Ann says, wringing her wet pigtail out.

But I have another idea. "Wait," I whisper, grabbing her hand and pulling her into the living room. "Now's my chance! Come with me."

"Chance for what?" Beth Ann asks suspiciously.

"Come on!" I tell her, taking the stairs two at a time. She follows reluctantly.

"Lace," she says as we stand outside Willa Dodge's bedroom door. "What are you up to?"

"The green suitcase," I remind her. "Willa's gone. Now we can search."

Her eyes widen, but she follows me inside. I peek into the closet, then kneel by the bed.

"It's just a bag. I don't see what the big deal is," Beth Ann whispers.

"There's something in there, something she's hiding," I whisper back. I reach into the darkness under the bed. There's no green suitcase, but my hand grazes something long. Something smooth. I pull it out. It's a large piece of paper, rolled up tight like a poster, secured with a green rubber band.

"Hey, look at this!"

Beth Ann hurries over. "It's a drawing," she says, watching as I unroll the paper. She's right. It's a sketch of a building. Like a floor plan. Only I recognize this floor plan.

"This is my house!"

"Yeah, here's your room." Beth Ann points to an up-stairs box. It's a handmade map of our house. The only detailed parts of the drawing are the doors. Every entry and exit is clearly marked in red pen. There are even measurements by each.

"Why is she mapping out your house?" Beth Ann asks.

"Why is she marking all the exits and entryways?"

"To find her way in?" Beth Ann shrugs.

"Or a quick way out. She's up to something and wants a quick getaway."

"May I help you?" We spin around. There in the door-way looms Willa Dodge. Her beady eyes dart back and forth from Beth Ann to me. We jump up, and I kick the map back under the bed.

"Um, just looking for something I lost," I stammer.

"Under my bed?"

Beth Ann squeezes my hand. Willa Dodge sits down on the bed. Her eyes narrow.

"Uh, well, it's Cinder. We lost Cinder!" Beth Ann al-most shouts.

"Under my bed?" Willa Dodge asks again.

I slap my forehead. It's getting worse.

"Yeah! He's stuck," Beth Ann rambles on. "Well, at least we thought he was stuck. He does that sometimes, gets stuck, that is. You know dogs. Not too bright," Beth Ann says, tapping her head matter-of-factly. "Now cats, they wouldn't do that. Cats are smart. Cats don't get stuck. At least not under beds. Though they do get stuck in trees sometimes. What about you, do you like cats?" she asks, her voice now shrill with nerves.

Willa Dodge stares incredulously at Beth Ann, her expression so full of confusion that I am suddenly grateful for my friend's crazy rant.

"Sorry, Mrs. Dodge," I interrupt before Beth Ann can go on any longer. "Didn't mean to disturb you." I shove Beth Ann into the hall.

"Good night," I yelp, slapping the door shut. I grab Beth Ann's hand and drag her down the hall to the safety of my own room. "What is the matter with you?" I hiss, once the door is closed behind us. "She's onto us. Now we'll never find that bag."

"Big deal," Beth Ann says, and shrugs. "Luggage is filthy. Do you know how many hands touch a single suitcase in any given airport? We've no idea where those bags have been. No idea at all."

"That's not the point, Beth Ann. What about that map? This whole thing is creepy. She's up to something, and we need to find that green bag now more than ever!"

"Are you gonna tell your dad?"

I picture Dad at his desk, on the phone with Mom, the furrow in his brow twitching. I can't tell him. It will only add to his worry.

"Not yet. I need more evidence." It's true. If I'm going to upset Dad, I need hard proof.

Beth Ann twirls her pigtails thoughtfully. "It may not be as bad as you think," she muses. "Maybe Willa just likes to draw? Maybe she's an architect? That's it! I'll bet she's an architect. And those are some plans she's working on. We should ask if she designed any famous buildings. Like the Eiffel Tower. Imagine that, the woman who designed the Eiffel Tower is living right here in your house!"

———

Later that night, after Beth Ann has gone home, Dad and I sit at the kitchen table and eat a bowl of ice cream. Fireflies bat at the window, blinking green and yellow before disappearing in the night. It feels strange that Willa Dodge is upstairs in our guest room. With a map of our house under her bed.

"So, what do you think?" Dad whispers, taking my empty bowl to the sink. "It's been a couple days."

"She's all right, I guess." I think of Willa Dodge bustling around Mom's kitchen like it's hers. And the businesslike way she whips through dinner, barely speaking to anyone.

"Dad?" I ask, joining him at the sink. "Does Mrs. Dodge know why she's here?"

"What do you mean? She's here to help out." He passes me a bowl to dry.

"No, Dad, I mean *why* we need her to help out. Does she know, about Mom and Marni?"

Dad pauses and stares at the dishcloth in his hand.

"Lace." He looks at me. "The agency trains people like her to help people like us."

People like us. It has come to that. Dad and I never talk about Marni. It's not that I really want to, but I don't like the fact that we don't. That there's somehow this silent agreement not to.

"Willa's a big help, Lace. And cooking and cleaning aren't all she does. She's going to be a big help after the homecoming."

I feel Dad's eyes on me, a sad weight that presses at my temples. "Can we just not talk about her?"

Dad nods. "Mom misses you," he says.

"She called already tonight?"

"This morning, while you were out walking Cinder. But she's probably home now, if you want to call her back."

"*This* is her home," I remind him.

I can hear Mom's old voice, soft and rippling like water. And how it sounds on the phone now. Not just far away. Different.

"Why don't you go see her? In Portland."

"No." I say it too loud and too fast. I think of winding roads and highways. I imagine her rented apartment with her bags unpacked. And then I think of Willa Dodge, here. In charge of Dad and Cinder.

"Let's wait until the end of July. Maybe Mom'll be home by then."

Dad sighs and shakes his head only slightly. "But, Lace, we don't really know—"

"Please, Dad," I interrupt. "The end of the month."

He nods. "Okay. The end of the month."

We finish the dishes in silence. When Dad goes up to his study, I pull the plug, staring into the sink at the suds swirling toward the drain. The spirals of soapy water start wide and slow, gurgling gently. As the sink empties, the spirals tighten, each swirl faster and louder, until the drain makes sucking noises, swallowing them down. I think of Marni then, and wonder if it was like that for her.

The Pie

Gran is out of the truck before Grampa has even pulled up to our door. When I look up from the beans I'm snapping, she is already scooting up the porch steps, a frenzied blur of outreached arms and bags.

"Lacey Bean!" she shrieks, gathering me up in the folds of her purple dress. She smells like butter and brown sugar, and I breathe in deeply. I am so relieved the Grands are here.

"Lord's sakes, Trudy, let the child breathe," Grampa yells from the driveway. He's holding one brown suitcase. Then I see the mountain of purple bags he's pulling from the truck. They roll out and scatter to the ground, as if they're leaping off the truck trying to catch up with Gran.

"Gol' dang," he mutters, but Gran doesn't notice.

"How's your dad?" she coos, and then, lowering her voice to a whisper, "And how's that Mrs. Dodge?" Her eyebrows flicker up and down.

"We're fine, Gran. Willa Dodge's in the kitchen making supper."

Gran's face goes serious. "And her pies? Can that woman make a peach pie like your grandma does?" I try to hide my smile, because Gran's peach pie is no laughing matter.

"No pies yet." This pleases her, and she claps her hands, her ruby rings clinking together.

"Well then, let's meet this woman." She sails past me, a purple blur.

At dinner we sit down and hold hands in a quick prayer. This is something we never did before, until this summer.

Gran passes me the salad. "Bean, how's that nice little friend of yours, what's her name? Beverly Annabelle?"

"You mean Beth Ann. She's good. She's going away with her family for three weeks in August."

"Is her father still making those god-awful contraptions?" Grampa asks.

"Luther," scolds Gran.

"Well, it's true. The last time we were here that poor kid was tripping down the street wearing some kind of glow-in-the-dark goggles, remember? Her father was testing out some kind of night vision thingy. And last Easter, didn't we see her shooting down the sidewalk in a pair of rocket-propelled roller skates, blue smoke streaming out the back?"

I nod.

"Like a blazing train wreck!" he exclaims.

"Oh yes," Gran says, and nods, remembering. "We all thought that poor girl was on fire."

"And wasn't it Mrs. Pringle who hosed her off?" Grampa asks.

"Rubbish, that old biddy loved the excuse to turn the hose on an innocent child."

"Old biddy?" Grampa chuckles. "Isn't Mrs. Pringle 'bout your age, honey bun?" He squeezes her cheek, and Gran waves him away. It's true about Beth Ann, though. Having three kids in the family gives her dad plenty of opportunity to test out all his inventions in his very own backyard. She never seems to mind, but I do feel kind of sorry for her.

"So how is that friend? Any burns or disfiguring scars?" Grampa asks.

"Luther!" Gran pokes him with her fork.

"She's fine," I say. "We've been going to Pratt Pool."

Grampa passes the chicken and shakes his head. "The pool? Now why on earth would ya go there?" He shakes a drumstick at Dad and me, and barbecue sauce splatters the tablecloth. "I will never understand why all you kids think it's such a nifty thing to dunk your heads in chlorine. Rots the brain, that pool water. Especially when you've got that great big lake out back!"

Dad looks at me sideways and shakes his head at Grampa. "Now, Dad, the kids enjoy both. The pool slide is fun. Right, Lace?"

I nod gratefully, because we both know I never spent much time at the pool until this summer.

For the rest of dinner everyone talks at once, and passes food, and chews and laughs, and you wouldn't even know Willa Dodge was at the table if it weren't for her looming shadow, blocking the sun from the window. She eats with her head down, businesslike, wrestling peas from their pods with quick, efficient bites. I sneak a peek for fangs.

"Willa," Gran says, leaning in like she's letting Willa Dodge in on a big secret, "how would you like a taste of the best peach pie north of Georgia? Made it myself just this morning."

If Willa's considering Gran's offer, she doesn't show it. Instead, Willa Dodge glances at Gran's ruby-ringed hand on her arm. I'll have to tell Gran to hide her jewels.

Determined, Gran leans in closer. "Let me tell you how I make it." She seizes the rest of dinner for a long account of how her peach pie was born, given as seriously as the State of the Union address. And we listen dutifully. Finally, Gran passes dessert plates around. She whisks each one down with a flourish, and I can see she's putting on a show. The peach pie will be the main event. Willa Dodge sets down her fork, dabs her mouth, and looks at Gran. Gran smiles back at her, holding out a heaping plate of pie.

"Well, here it is," she announces, as though the guest of honor has just arrived. I'm not sure if it's an offering or a challenge. We all hold our breath.

But Willa Dodge shakes her head. "No, thank you. Don't really care for peach," she says, rising from the table.

Grampa and Dad lean back in their chairs, as if preparing for a big wind. Gran's mouth drops open, and Willa Dodge, appearing not to notice, starts clearing the table. The pie tastes a little bitter that night.

Later I find Gran rocking in the dark on the front porch. Her purple dress is settled around her like a giant grape puddle.

"G'night, Gran," I say.

She stares at the fireflies, head shaking left and right.

"I don't understand," she murmurs. "What kind of woman doesn't like peach pie?"

The Practice

Monday morning is Beth Ann's first swim lesson with the novice class. And I am already late.

"See you later!" I shout as I run through the kitchen. Grampa's left arm shoots out from where he's sitting at the breakfast table. He scoops me up into one of his bear hugs, as if I am still just five years old.

"Lookee here what I caught! A rare and vicious species. I do believe it's a lake rat!"

Dad winks over his newspaper.

"Where you off to so fast, Bean?" Gran wants to know.

"I'm meeting Beth Ann at her swimming lesson," I say, and giggle, wiggling out of Grampa's squeeze.

"You heading down to the lake?" Grampa asks. "I'd love to join you. A little dippety-doo would do this old body some good!"

"Why that sounds like a fine idea!" Dad chimes in, sitting up straight in his chair.

All three look at me with such hope in their eyes. I hate to disappoint them.

"Um, I'm not going to the lake. Lessons are at the pool."

"But where's your swimsuit?" Grandma wants to know.

"I'm not swimming today," I say, fiddling with my

knapsack. "It's not that hot out, and besides, I just like to draw while Beth Ann practices."

Dad sinks back in his chair, and Grampa pulls his mustache uncomfortably. This information bothers them. But Gran rescues us all.

"Well, you be sure to show me your drawings when you get back. Scoot, now. I've got a banana cream pie to make." She rubs her hands together excitedly. "That'll knock the old broad's socks off!"

"Used to be I knocked your socks off," Grampa teases, turning on a wicked grin.

"Oh shoo, you crazy old man," Gran says with a chuckle.

As I jog down our driveway, the lake spreads beside me. Across the street the beach is already filling with swimmers, and I have to admit the sand looks inviting, compared to the concrete patio and tiny grass strip around the town pool. But still I cut right, across Main Street and down Pratt. I have gotten pretty good at passing the lake without looking. Just as I ignore the swim meets that take place there on the weekends. The first meet was the worst. I had been eating breakfast on the back porch as the buses began to pull in from neighboring towns, before I realized what I was watching. I was unable to move as the opposing teams strolled across the sand, dropping their bags on picnic tables, stretching before heading down to the docks for each heat. When I couldn't watch any more, I hurried up to my room, closing the windows against the cheering crowd. The horns that blew to signal each start gripped me with a nausea I couldn't contain. That was the first meet, a few weeks ago. It hasn't gotten much easier since, but I've learned to turn my music up loud inside my bedroom on meet days, or make plans to be at Beth Ann's house, away from the water. Anything to dull the roar of the lake outside my window.

———

Marni was always the first one up on summer mornings, and she'd be in her swimsuit at the breakfast table, goggles draped around her neck. Just after the rest of us straggled into the kitchen, she'd be out the door and on her bike, pedaling off to practice. I'd find her at the lake, practice long over, and she'd be stretched out on a dock or sitting in the sand with her friends, hair pulled back, still wet. I can't look at the docks without seeing her lean shape tucked into diving form, a shadow above the water before slicing its glassy surface.

Mom, Dad, and I always watched the swim meets together. Noisy buses from all over the county arrived for the competition. Small crowds gathered on the foggy beach, the sun still making its way up in the sky. The lake looked different then. Fog rose off its green surface, and the shore was gray and still. Those mornings Marni was quiet. She complained when Mom made her eat something, her stomach a net of butterflies. We knew to leave her alone.

"Let her get her fins wet," Mom would say.

It was true. When the whistle blew, Marni lined up on the dock with the other swimmers. It didn't matter if we waved or Dad called her name for a picture, like the other families. Unlike her teammates, seeking out and mouthing nervous words to parents, Marni didn't seem to hear us. Instead, she perched at the edge, toes curled over the dock, head bowed in concentration. She stood silent in the line of swimmers, far away from them, and from us. When the horn sounded, she slipped into the water. Out in front, arms steady, propelling her body down the lane. Once she was in the water, it happened. Her long arms moved easily, effortlessly. Where other kids kicked and splashed, Marni's wake was still. She slipped through the dark currents like a seal, silent and steady, a gentle ripple her only trail. We held our breath. Only when she surfaced at the other dock, wide eyes searching for the time on the starter's clock, did she smile. And then she'd wave, finding our faces in the crowd. Someone always pulled her from the water, sleek and glistening. Wrapped in a towel, she'd trot back down the dock grinning. Returning to the beach, and to us. Only then was she ours again.

Freestyle

"You don't breathe when you're underwater!" the exasperated coach cries.

Below her, floundering in the shallow end of the pool, Beth Ann surfaces. Her goggles are crooked, her red pigtails stuck to her face. She sputters, and pool water shoots from her mouth like a fountain.

The coach shakes her head wearily. "Let's take a break." It's hard to tell who needs it more.

I kneel by the edge. "How's it going?"

"Lace, is that you?" Beth Ann turns her head left, then right, like a blind bat.

"Oh no, those aren't special swim goggles your dad made, are they?"

Beth Ann smiles. "It is you! Yeah, these are Dad's improved underwater vision goggles!"

"And they don't work, do they?"

"Well, they are a little blurry," she admits.

"Isn't all this difficult enough already?" I ask. "That's it. I'm bringing you a pair of real swimmer's goggles."

I give her my arm and help her out of the pool.

"Yeah, you're probably right," she agrees, flopping on the pool deck beside me.

A chorus of splashes erupts behind us. We both turn. At the far end of the pool, the Summer Trout team jumps in and begins their practice laps in the adjoining lanes. The swimmers cut even strokes through the water and barrel toward us. Beth Ann looks away.

"Don't worry," I assure her. "You'll be down there soon."

A tall, tan leader gathers a smaller group in a circle in the far lane, where the water is shallow. Sully Tanner. He's showing some younger students the freestyle stroke. Marni's stroke. We watch him circle his arms above his head, first left, then right, as he turns his head to demonstrate the breath. These kids are much younger than Beth Ann.

"Stroke, stroke, breathe," his voice echoes across the pool. My tummy squirms just hearing him.

"That's what I have trouble with," Beth Ann mumbles.

"I know who can help." Something comes over me, and before I can change my mind, I'm heading his way. Sully Tanner looks up.

"Um, my friend is new to this, and she's having a little trouble, and . . ."

Sully smiles. "The Watts girl?" Once again, everyone knows Beth Ann.

"Yeah. Could you maybe help her with her stroke?"

"No problem. Anything for Lace Martin's friend." His white teeth glow above the blue pool water.

I stare until I can feel the red creeping up my neck and

into my checks. My face is still burning as I rush back to tell Beth Ann the news.

"Oh my God. He's coming over here? To help *me*?" She is starting to choke.

"Yeah," I say. "Sully Tanner is coming to help you."

But he smiled at me, I think.

The Cook-off

It's the second week of July, and the summer heat presses on my temples as I ride my bike home from the pool. For just a moment I allow myself to imagine slipping into Pratt Pool with Beth Ann, and a watery relief starts to flow over me. But then I catch myself. By the time I wheel my bike up to the house, I am drenched. I lean the bike against the porch steps and peer through the screen door. In the kitchen, Dad and Gran and Grampa Martin hover around the sink. At first Willa Dodge is nowhere to be seen, but then I spot her. From under the counter, two stockinged legs stick out. Like the wicked witch under Dorothy's house! I watch, in awe.

There is some grunting, a loud clang, and Willa Dodge emerges, wrench in hand.

"All fixed," she announces, wiping her hands matter-of-factly on her apron.

"You fixed it? So quickly?" Dad is shocked. "But how?"

Willa shrugs. "With this." She waves the wrench and disappears into the laundry room. It looks like Dad finally gave up and let her have a try.

"That sure is some woman," Grampa says, with a long, low whistle.

"Oh, you be quiet, you old coot," Gran warns.

Dad crosses his arms and smiles, clearly impressed. "Amazing! I don't know what we'd do without her."

This annoys me, and I'm about to push open the screen door and remind him that Mom's coming home soon when Gran interrupts.

"Have you thought any more about hiring a nurse, for when she comes home?" She ushers Dad and Grampa to the table and moves to the stove, where I can see her turn on the kettle. I press myself against the outside wall and slide down. I peer in to see how Dad answers.

Dad shakes his head. "I don't want it to feel like a clinic around here. We've had enough nurses and therapists. That's where Willa comes in."

"Willa?" Gran sounds surprised. "Dear, house help isn't going to be enough. She'll need more than that."

"I know," Dad assures her. "That's why I hired Willa. She's worked as both a caregiver and a domestic helper. The agency assures me she's had plenty of experience with the kind of transition we're going to experience."

I shudder at the word. We've had enough transition

already. This was to be a homecoming, a family reunion. Not a transition. I close my eyes and press my forehead against the screen door until it hurts.

"I hope you're right," Gran says, shaking her head worriedly.

"Me, too," Dad allows.

It's quiet for a moment, the slow hiss of the teakettle heating up the only noise in the house, until Grampa slaps the table decidedly. "We're doing all right," he says firmly. "This family has had about all it can stand, and I say we're doing all right. There's a few adjustments we need to make around the house, but we'll do it." He reaches for Gran's hand and sets his gently on hers.

"We're doing the best we can," she agrees. "But I'm still worried about Lace."

My chest tightens, and I turn my ear to the door so I can hear better.

"She hasn't been back in the lake?"

"Not even to the beach," Dad says.

"Then it's time for a Martin family fishing trip," Grampa offers.

"I disagree," Gran says. Her voice is firm. "When she's ready she'll go, and it's not up to us when that will be."

Finally, someone is on my side. I smile at her from the doorway, and she must feel it because she looks up.

"Well, there's my girl! How 'bout some tea?" Everyone

at the table turns, suddenly smiling and lively, and they begin bustling about. If they think it's strange that I'm crouched out on the porch, no one mentions it. Instead, Grampa opens the screen door and ushers me in. Gran fetches two teacups. Dad crawls under the sink to marvel at Willa's work. I open my beach bag and climb onto a stool with my sketchbook.

"What're you working on there?" Gran asks, pulling Mom's recipe box from a drawer.

"Pratt Pool."

She peers over my shoulder. In a whirl of aqua blues, a red-haired girl with green goggles paddles fiercely. I even made motion marks and sprays of water to show the action.

"Oh, my," Gran remarks. "Looks like someone I know. How did the lesson go?" I consider telling Gran about Sully Tanner and how smoothly he glides from one end of the pool to the other. I want to ask her if she knows the school swim record is his, for both the men's freestyle and the butterfly. And that he can do a double backflip off the high board. But then I look down at the red-haired dog paddler sputtering on the page and a wave of guilt washes over me. So I tell her about Beth Ann's progress. Even though I leave out the part that she's in the beginner's class with the kindergartners, Gran clucks her tongue.

"That poor child." The teakettle whistles, and Gran

fills our cups. "Willa?" she calls. "I make a mean cup of chamomile."

Willa Dodge emerges from the laundry room with a basket and shakes her head.

Gran sighs. "Honestly! What kind of woman doesn't like a bit of tea in the afternoon?"

Grampa just shakes his head, settling himself at the table with the newspaper.

Since the peach pie incident the day before, Gran's been trying out dishes for Willa Dodge. In just twenty-four hours, she's pulled out all the favorites from our family history, leaving no relative's recipe uncooked. First she made Aunt Jenny's rice pudding for breakfast. Willa Dodge only grunted. So she tried Cousin Elda's corn chowder for lunch. Willa Dodge raised one eyebrow. Gran wasn't used to this, and it made her a little loony. She's spent all day rifling through Mom's recipe files in search of the One. At one point I think Gran had reached so far up into the family tree that she was just about teetering on the tallest branch waving her wooden spoon.

But now she's found it. "It's lemon muffins for her," Gran declares, slapping down the recipe card on the table.

Grampa and I keep vigil, he with his paper and I with my sketchbook. For the next hour, the whole kitchen hums in the wake of Gran's determination.

"Whoo-ee, Jemima," Grampa coos as the room fills with the scent of citrus. "When the dust settles, how about a little taste for your muffin over here?"

Gran spins around in a cloud of flour. "You watch it, Luther. This cooking's not for the likes of you!"

As soon as the muffins pop, Gran corners Willa Dodge in the living room. "I've got something you won't be able to resist!" she declares.

Grampa and I move to the doorway to watch. Gran's silver hair is tangled like a birds' nest and her clothes are splattered with flour, but she has the wild look of triumph about her. Grampa and I wait, listening.

"What's she saying?" he whispers hoarsely in my ear. I shake my head.

Willa Dodge accepts the muffin, and Gran jiggles on her tiptoes while Willa chews away. For a long time Willa smacks and tastes, and the longer she does, the wider Gran's smile becomes. Surely this is it. She can now put away her apron.

From the doorway, we hear Willa Dodge's loud swallow and watch as Gran practically swoons in anticipation. But she will have to wait.

Willa sets the muffin down and picks up the laundry she's been folding. "Needs sugar," she says, lumbering past Gran and up the stairs.

Grampa and I scramble back to the table.

"Run for cover, kiddo!" he shouts.

I try not to giggle as Gran returns, throwing open cupboard doors, plucking fresh pans from the shelf. Grampa sashays over and gets himself a plate.

"So, how 'bout a lemon muffin for your sweet muffin?"

Gran doesn't even look up. She snatches the plate away from him, yanks up the window, and tosses the muffins right out to the birds.

"Put a lid on it, Luther," she warns. "Get your muffin-loving bottom over here and help me clean the mixer. It's chocolate mousse for her!"

Cleaning

I know something is wrong as soon as I see Marni's open door. Someone is moving about inside the room. Then I realize it must be Dad. And I am relieved, because he's finally decided to go in.

As I tiptoe past, I sneak a glance. There, in the middle of the room, is a vacuum cleaner, the cord uncoiled on the rug. Something else is different. My eyes roam the room, checking things off. The magazines by the bed, the jeans on the chair. Everything looks the same. Except the dresser. It looks oddly empty. And then I realize what it is. Marni's swim trophies are gone.

Just then the bathroom door flies open, and it's not Dad. It's Willa Dodge with an armload of Marni's laundry.

"You can't be in here!" I want to yell. I open my mouth to tell her to put Marni's clothes down, to get out, but all that comes out is a painful squeak. Suddenly my throat feels tight like it did at the pool, and my eyes fill with tears. All I can do is stand there clenching my fists, shaking my head back and forth.

Willa Dodge frowns at me and puts the clothes down. "What's the matter?" she asks.

Suddenly Dad appears in the door behind me and pushes gently past, arms out. "I'm sorry, Mrs. Dodge, this room isn't to be cleaned. Please, just leave everything as it is. It's my fault for not explaining." Willa Dodge looks back and forth between the two of us. We must be a sight: Dad's face pinched with worry and apology, my own red with rage and tears. She winds up the vacuum cord, leaving the clothes behind on the floor. My breath comes back to me in deep gulps and the tears slow. Dad ushers us out, vacuum in hand, gently closing the door behind us.

"Her trophies," I whisper, but he shakes his head as if to say, *Not now.*

The Warning

"I did it! I killed her with chocolate," Gran says as she waves her cookbook victoriously the next morning at breakfast.

"You did what?" I ask, tossing my beach bag on the table.

"My chocolate mousse. It won Willa over. She even asked for the recipe!"

Grampa snorts from behind his newspaper. "I believe she asked who made it."

"That's just the same. What more can you expect from a woman who dislikes peach pie?"

Grampa smacks the paper on the table. "Well, that storm may have passed, but according to the weatherman there's another on the way tonight," he reports. "A real whammy. Wind gusts, thunder, the works! We'd better get your dad on his way before it hits," he warns.

The Grands are staying on with me while Dad heads back to Portland. It is his third trip without me, and I know he's not happy about my decision to stay home.

"Well, I hope he's packed by now," Gran says. "He's been up there over an hour."

"I'll go get him," I offer, and I grab an apple from the fruit bowl before running upstairs to find Dad. But he's not packing his suitcase in his room. Instead I find him seated at his desk, staring wearily at the stacks of work spread across it.

"Can I talk to you?"

His brow is furrowed in concentration as he moves paper from one stack to another and then back. He sighs. "What is it, honey?"

"Where's Willa?" I ask, looking up and down the hall.

"At the market."

Good. I clear my throat. "I need to tell you something, Dad."

Now he looks concerned. He takes off his glasses.

"The other night, around midnight, something strange woke me up."

"Was it a bad dream?"

"No, Dad, this was different. Someone was sneaking in and out of the house. It was Willa Dodge. She'd been out in the middle of the night. At the lake."

"How do you know she was down at the lake?"

"The hallway was wet. She dripped."

"Willa dripped?" he asks, placing his glasses back on. He doesn't seem terribly alarmed. "Well, that's just silly. Maybe she'd taken a late shower or something."

"No, Dad, it wasn't shower water. She left a muddy trail down the hall. I wanted to show you, but she erased it before I could."

"She *erased* it?" This news does not have the effect I

expected. Dad frowns and readjusts his glasses. "Lace, maybe she went for a late swim. Either way, you shouldn't be spying on her. Now, I have to finish this project."

"But, Dad, that's not all. She has a map! A map of our house, with all the doorways marked. It's hidden under her bed."

Dad smiles, a tired smile that doesn't quite fill up his face. "Lace, this is silly. She's helping us get the house ready. It's part of her job."

"I don't care what her job is. The point is she's not who you think she is!"

"Enough. We will discuss this later, when I get back from Portland."

"Later?" I shout. "But later is too late! I think she's stealing stuff. Your watch disappeared, and now Marni's trophies are gone, too! You can't leave with all this going on."

Dad slaps his pencil down and puts his head in his hands. He is surrounded by piles of paper and blueprints, and he sinks behind them like the sun going down behind a mountain.

"Lace, I have to tidy up this paperwork before I get on the road." His voice is firm but he is not shouting, because Dad never shouts. He never slams doors or stomps out of rooms.

So I do.

I cross my arms and stomp my feet as hard as I can. I stomp all the way down the hall and downstairs. I make sure to stomp each step louder than the one before, so that by the time I get to the bottom, my feet are pounding and the floor vibrates beneath me. And I don't stop there. I storm past Gran, wide-eyed at the kitchen table.

Grampa looks up. "Whoo-ee, that storm's come early. And right here in our very own kitchen!"

Gran elbows him and reaches out to me, but I am already through the door with a final slam. I hear Grampa hoot behind it.

Cinder trots worriedly behind me. I take the leash gently from his mouth, and he smiles just a little, so that only his front teeth show. I stroke his ears and rub his face until I see all his teeth.

"Don't worry," I tell him. "Maybe Dad's too busy to listen. But Mom'll be home soon, and before she is I'll find that green suitcase."

The Invite

The pool is packed with hot kids and weary-looking parents, so I wait by the snack bar while Beth Ann suits up.

Marni's friends Alex and Jennifer are across the pool, stretching before practice. I wave at them, and they smile, but neither one comes over. I know they don't mean to hurt my feelings, but it's still weird. They are her best friends, after all. Dad says people do strange things when they're hurting. He says sometimes it's easier for people to keep their distance. But it makes me feel like nothing more than a shadow, as if seeing me is nothing more than a dark reminder of Marni being gone.

"She's back!" someone says brightly. It's Sully Tanner. I'm not sure if it's his smile or the sun, but suddenly I have to shade my eyes. "Let me buy you an ice cream."

"Sure," I stammer, scanning the flavors on the chalkboard. My stomach swirls, but I'm not about to say no. "I'll have vanilla."

"Vanilla? I thought you Martin girls were more daring. Maybe rocky road or peppermint swirl?"

A few older boys from the swim team crowd around. They are full of themselves, pushing and laughing. Until they see me. A quiet falls on the group, an air of seriousness that doesn't belong to a summer day. First it's Devon Willis, a tall, dark-haired boy from Marni's class. He glances at me and smiles uncomfortably. I notice his braces are gone, and I focus on his straight, white teeth. "Hey, Lace."

"Hi," I say.

"Real sorry about your sister," he stammers, looking suddenly at the ground. The others around him nod in agreement, their eyes roaming the pool deck.

Robbie Smith is next. "Swim team sucks without her this year!" he says too loudly. The others frown, and one elbows him in the side.

"What?" Robbie asks, rubbing his side. "It does."

"C'mon, guys," another says, nodding toward the pool. "Practice time."

"Ignore it," Sully tells me. "They don't know what to say."

I nod, because it's what always happens. But it's different with Sully watching. I feel exposed.

He touches my hand. It's only for a moment, but his skin is warm, his grasp gentle. "Are you going to the bonfire on Saturday night?" he asks.

My mind whirls. I see burning logs, glowing faces crowding together. The same bonfires Marni went to every weekend, the ones Mom said I wasn't old enough to join yet. But this summer is different. I imagine hot dogs roasting and music playing as the lake laps the shore. The lake. Suddenly I can't think straight.

"No. Yes. I mean, let me ask my dad. But I'm sure it'll be okay." It's Wednesday, I think. I have a few days to think about this.

"Sounds good," he says. "Bring a friend if you want." He waves and trots over to the pool, to his young swimmer fans, to googly-eyed Beth Ann teetering on the edge in her life preserver.

The Plan

The Wattses' yard is what you'd call a giant playground, but a very dangerous one. There are blue kiddie pools and wooden ramps spread across the grass and sandboxes, and trampolines where you'd normally expect to find flower beds and walkways. In fact, there's no real yard amid the clutter. You have to hop or wiggle to get through it. From down the street, the yard looks exciting, like a carnival. But upon closer inspection, you see that this is not a playground for kids. In fact, it's not a playground at all. It's a testing zone for Mr. Watts's newfangled inventions and experiments, and at any time explosions might erupt from various areas.

The truth comes up close. What appears to be a sandbox is a dirt field for small rockets to be fired from, and a landing zone for those that crash—most of them do. The ramp area, the one I find most scary, is where the rocket-propelled roller skate was first tested. And most recently, I imagine, the double-wide purple bike tires. The kiddie pools are underwater labs where high-speed fins and X-ray goggles are tested, usually by Beth Ann or Mr. Watts himself. Often you can find him in his swimsuit kneeling in a kiddie pool with his snorkel in place.

"What on earth must the neighbors think?" my mother used to ask.

Beth Ann is crouching by the garage when I pedal up.

"What are you doing?" I ask.

"Lace!" she cries. "Get out of the way, quick!"

Suddenly the sky darkens, and Beth Ann points up. Darting down the slope of the roof is Mr. Watts in a red bodysuit, outstretched arms strapped to what appears to be a giant kite.

"Dad's trying out his new roof glider." Beth Ann's voice doesn't quiver when she says this, and she focuses on the large stopwatch in her hand. But I can't tear my eyes from the roof. Mr. Watts trots down the peak, gaining speed up to the very edge. He hesitates for only a second, then leaps high and wide over Mrs. Watts's shrubs. Beth Ann clicks the watch, and we both stare at the yellow-winged figure above us, circling above the kiddie pools and flying almost gracefully over the branches of neighboring trees. He glides slowly left, then right, when suddenly he halts in midair.

"Oh-oh."

Mr. Watts gains speed, no longer going up but down.

"Left, Dad, swing left!" Beth Ann shouts. I see the large trampoline she's pointing to and will Mr. Watts to turn left. Just when I think he's a goner, the kite jerks left and he lands with a giant *whump* in the center of the trampoline.

Beth Ann races over. "Thirty seconds, Dad, thirty seconds! The best time yet!" she exclaims.

Mr. Watts rolls off the trampoline and lies on the ground panting. My own knees feel a little weak, but Mrs. Watts pops casually out the window with a plate of treats.

"Oh, hi there, Lacey," she says. "Want some super-duper-glider brownies? They're organic!" Like I said, a giant carnival.

Upstairs in her room, Beth Ann and I gobble up the brownies.

"Promise me you will never test that glider thingy, okay?" I demand, licking chocolate from my fingers.

"Oh, Dad would never let me. Too dangerous." Beth Ann thrusts a disinfectant wipe into my hands, but I've already licked them clean.

"I washed them earlier," I lie. I know she doesn't believe me, but oddly enough she rolls onto her back and smiles at the ceiling.

"After practice today Sully said, 'Hope to see you Saturday!' Can you believe we're going to a bonfire with Sully Tanner?"

"Well, we're not exactly going with him, Beth Ann. He's going to be there, is all."

"But he asked us!"

"Yeah, and about fifty other kids, too." I say this, but really I'm secretly as excited as Beth Ann. Even if she thinks he asked her first.

"I need to find out more about Willa Dodge, and I need your help. Can you sleep over after the bonfire?"

"Oh, Lace. You've got to stop with this Willa stuff," she says, and looks out the window at her winged father. Mr. Watts is still in his red flight suit, scribbling notes on a clipboard. He doesn't seem to notice the crowd of neighbors who've gathered in the yard.

"Of course, we'll go to the bonfire first," I say, trying to entice her. "Sully Tanner will be looking for us." I know this is not true. Dad would say I'm taking advantage of a friend, but it works.

"Oh, why not," she says as she grabs another brownie. "But only after we go to the bonfire!"

Lost

Early Friday morning, Gran's purple bags are lined up on the porch. The truck is pulled around to the back door. Dad has just returned home, and now it is the Grands' turn to drive to Portland.

"Are you sure you won't come?" Gran asks.

"We'll have you there by nightfall. Your ma would love to see you," Grampa adds.

"I'll be fine here," I say, ducking the invitation.

"Well, I hope Portland is ready for us." Gran wraps herself around me like an octopus.

"Lord, Trudy, let that child up for air." Grampa pulls my ear and plants a firm kiss on my head before he hops in the truck.

"Have a good trip," Dad tells them. "Call as soon as you get there."

"Wait!" Gran cries, looking at her hand. "My rings. My ruby rings are missing!"

My heart leaps. Willa Dodge can't escape this one.

Gran is scrambling through her bags, plucking them off the back of the truck.

"Well, ding dang, Trudy. It only took us three hours to pack this here stuff up. Now let's just yank it all out so we can do it again."

"But, Luther, my rings."

Dad joins in, searching through the nearest purple bag to land at his feet. Grampa bends over the mess.

"I know where they are!" I cry out over the noise. "I know who stole them."

"*Stole* them?" Dad asks, standing up. "Who said anyone stole them?"

Gran is still rifling through bags, not listening, but I have Dad's and Grampa's attention now.

"*She* did," I yell, pointing up to the guest room window. "Willa Dodge has Gran's rings!"

Found

I race for the house. It's then that I realize Willa Dodge is upstairs. She may have heard us. She may be escaping out the bedroom window right now. Or heading downstairs to this very room. I tear out the door with the phone.

But no one looks alarmed. No one thanks me and dials 911. Instead, they are calmly packing the truck back up, replacing each purple bag.

"What's going on?"

"Oh, there you are." Gran is all smiles. "Look what was in my pocket after all!" She holds up her ruby rings.

"Lordy, Trudy, I think you did it on purpose just to see me pack up the truck again so you could admire my muscles." Grampa shakes his head and climbs back into the cab.

"They were in your pocket?" I ask in disbelief.

"Sure were, sugar. Now we gotta hit the road."

"But maybe someone stole them, and then felt bad and put them in your pocket. Someone close to you, like Willa Dodge."

Gran frowns at me. "Why on earth would Willa do that?" she asks.

"Because she's not who you think she is," I yell at all of them. "Willa Dodge is dangerous!" I plunge ahead. "I've been watching her. She sneaks around the house at night, looking for stuff to steal, like Dad's watch. And she's got this green suitcase, and I think she's hiding the loot in there. Plus, she drew a map of our house, and it's under the bed. Oh, and the trophies! Now Marni's trophies are missing." I'm talking so fast I have to stop for a breath, and by then Dad is at my side.

"Not this again," he says with a sigh.

"What is this child talking about?" Gran asks, her voice loud and alarmed. She's upset now, and Grampa leans across the steering wheel to hear what's going on.

"Lace has an active imagination, Mom. I keep trying to tell her there's nothing to worry about." Dad's voice is gentle, but I can tell he's losing his patience. I look up at his calm face, and I want to shake him. I want to pull him by his collared shirt and yell, *I think we have a situation!*

"He's wrong. Dad is just too nice. He doesn't see her for what she is," I protest. I can't tell if Gran believes me, but she is listening and her eyes are soft.

"And what is she, honey?"

"A criminal." I blurt it out.

The adults are looking at each other now, and Grampa turns off the engine and comes around the truck. He leans against it like we have all the time in the world.

"Bean. I know what you're thinking," he says.

"You do?" Gran, Dad, and I say at once.

"Yes. That Willa Dodge is an unusual woman. But I have my own idea what's really going on."

Thank God for Grampa. He is the only one who gets it. I sink against Dad and prepare to listen patiently as he explains to them how smart I am, how observant and wise. They will be thanking me afterward, saying, "Lace, how could we have doubted you? How could we not have known?" I look at Dad and hope he's listening.

"You see," Grampa continues, "a person like Willa Dodge comes into your life when things are a little messy. Things are different around here this summer, and even though she's here to help, she's something different, too. Sometimes when things get messy, a person can't recognize their life anymore, can't even recognize themself. We get crazy notions. So we look around at all the mess that needs fixin' and we reach for the first thing we see. And we try to fix that, because tryin' to fix it makes us feel a little bit better. It takes our mind off things a while.

"Now I wouldn't vote Willa Dodge for friendliest-person award, but I know your dad loves you and would never have someone here who's dangerous. And I know her help is important. It frees us up to get our tools together, to pick up what we do recognize in this mess, and sort through the rubble. And most important, I know she's here to do something special."

Special? Willa Dodge? Grampa was my last hope, but she's even got him fooled.

"I mean it, Lace. There's some things you don't know yet, that you may not be ready for. But you will eventually. This'll all make sense in the end." He pats my head. "You've got the right idea, Bean. Things do need fixing. You just want to be sure what you're aiming to fix is what's really broke to begin with."

The air around us presses in, and the light reflecting off the lake burns. This is not what I had in mind. Grampa is not talking to Gran or Dad; this is meant for me. And I'm not sure yet what he means, but I don't like the sound of it.

Dad squeezes my shoulder gently, and Gran takes my face in her hands. She's crying a little, and I think it's probably not just because she's saying goodbye. Grampa winks before hopping back in the truck. Soon they're rattling down the driveway, a trail of hot dust rising behind in the morning. When Dad and I turn toward the house, something flutters above us. Behind the curtains in the guest room window is the round face of Willa Dodge. Looking down at me.

The Call

On Saturday, Dad agrees to let me go to the bonfire. Just like that. There is no concern, no questions about who will be there, or what time I will be home. Dad looks worried and distracted, and as wrong as I know it is, I am actually glad. We have not spoken much about his trip. Last night at dinner, without the noise and company of the Grands, was the perfect time. But Dad seemed exhausted, and the only thing I wanted to know was if anything had changed.

At that his face clouded, and he shook his head sadly. "No," he said. And that was the end of it.

But tonight, just as I am getting ready to meet Beth Ann, Dad enters the kitchen with the phone in his hand. He twists the pencil behind his ear, round and round. "It's your mom." He seems happy and worried at the same time.

It's hard to tell if this is good news or not.

"Hi, Mom," I say, cradling the phone protectively.

"Lacey, how's my girl?"

"Okay. What about you guys?"

"We're fine. It's so good to see your grandparents. I wish you were here, too."

"Are you coming home with them?"

"Not quite yet. We think it's time you come here."

"But, Mom."

Her voice is firm. "It's time, honey. Daddy comes each week. We want you to come with him the next time."

I listen quietly to all she has to say, though I don't say anything back. I can feel Dad beside me, hovering, listening. It's like the walls are closing in.

"I'll call you later," I tell Mom. "I can't talk about this any more right now." I hang up the phone and head for the door.

I'm outside and across the porch before Dad catches up. I hear him run out behind me, but I don't turn around. Let him puff, let him stammer. I'm not budging on this one.

"Lace, we've been talking about this for the past few weeks. I go each week. Gran and Grampa Martin are there. It's your turn now."

"I won't do it, Dad. I won't go."

Dad rests his hand on my shoulder, turning me to face him. His eyes water. "The first time, I didn't want to go either, honey. And yet nothing could've kept me away. You'll see for yourself. It'll be okay."

"It's not okay," I sob. "Don't you see? You walk around here like nothing's changed. Like they're on a trip or something. You do your work, you eat your dinner, and you ask me how the pool was. You put on your nice shirt and your pressed tie every day, but you don't even go into the office anymore. Don't you see how screwed up this is?" Tears are streaming down my face, but I don't care.

"Let's just calm down." Dad hands me his hand- kerchief, but I toss it on the ground.

"Look at us, Dad! Look at Cinder, at me, at Gran and Grampa. None of us will ever be the same!" I'm screaming now and I'm sure the neighbors can hear, but I don't feel like calming down. So I cry until I sink to the porch floor and can't cry anymore.

And then Dad surprises me. He loosens his tie and lies down on the boards beside me, unfolding like an old wooden deck chair. With both hands he covers his face. Suddenly I'm afraid I've made him cry. Instead he takes several long breaths, slow and deep, like little waves going in and out. I concentrate on these until my own chest begins to slow. We lie like this a long time, the waves moving in and out, in and out of us.

"You're right," he says, finally. "You are absolutely right."

I don't want to be right. Whenever I used to fight with Marni or Mom, I always wanted to win. I wanted to hear the words, to have them tell me I was right. But not this time. Cinder presses against me, and I turn in to his fur, burying my face in his scruffy neck. I can't look at Dad. Instead I look at Cinder, into his deep brown eyes. They are large and worried and full of love. He misses Marni, too.

Above us a summer breeze tousles tree branches. Clouds whirl in its wake. When Dad reaches out to pet Cinder, our hands meet across the soft span of his black back.

"I'll think about it," I whisper.

The Bonfire

"Are you sure about this?" Beth Ann pulls her pigtails nervously as we stand at the edge of the beach parking lot. She's been surveying the scene, and she eyes me warily now. "After all, aren't these high school kids?"

But that's not what worries me. Up ahead the beach glows, almost flickers against the pale stretch of lake behind it. I look out at the water and take a deep breath as I step onto the sand.

Already a large group is gathered around the fire, some laughing loudly, some drinking soda, a few bobbing to music. The faces shine with the firelight against the darkness, and I recognize them as we draw closer. Some of Marni's friends wave, as do several swim team members who smile as we pass them. The music is loud, and the smell of hot dogs fills my nose as we move toward the fire. Everyone is having a good time. Beth Ann comes to life.

"Wow!" she yelps, reaching out to pinch me. "Am I glad we came. Wasn't it nice of Sully to invite me? Wasn't it nice he said I could bring you along?"

I nod in the dark. Poor Beth Ann doesn't realize she's got it all backward. At least she left her double-wide purple-tired bike at my house. It took a lot of convincing, but when I see Jade Winslow and her friends, I know it was worth it. They stare in our direction.

"You made it," Sully says, strolling over to us, his swim jersey draped loosely over his shoulders. I'm not sure if this party is his or not, but he welcomes us like it is. "Want a soda?" He's asking me, but Beth Ann grabs the can from his hand.

"Thanks!" She grins widely. "Can I get another for my friend here?"

Sully raises his eyebrows but smiles anyway. "Of course, allow me."

Beth Ann beams, and I like him even more for this kindness.

We drink our sodas by the fire. It's a loud group, but whenever Sully speaks, I notice that other conversations grow quiet. Though he doesn't seem to notice this.

"It's like he owns the beach," Beth Ann whispers. Even the flames of the fire dance in his direction. A few girls from Marni's class stop to say hi. Alex and Jennifer wave me over, but I just wave back and pretend to be in deep conversation with Beth Ann. They start to head our way, but I'm relieved when they move on to greet a new-comer. Beth Ann hasn't said much this evening. Instead she sits mesmerized on our log, staring across the flames as some of the kids pair up and sway to the music of a slow song.

"Having fun?" Sully seats himself between us on the log, and Beth Ann scoots closer to him.

"It's nice," I answer, and I mean it. Beth Ann and I don't know everyone, but Sully has made sure to include us. He hands us each a hot dog and smiles at Beth Ann.

"I got one for your friend here, too."

I try not to giggle. When she excuses herself to get a napkin, Sully turns to me. His eyes glow like warm blue puddles in the firelight. I have to look away.

"I'm really glad you came, Lace."

"Me, too."

"Marni hung out here all the time."

Hearing her name, I brace my stomach for the familiar wave of worry that accompanies it, but it doesn't come this time.

"She loved this place. The team, the beach, the lake. She belongs here." Sully gets a far-off look in his eyes. Even though I don't want to think about her right now, I nod. It feels good to talk to Sully Tanner about swimming and Marni. And me.

"Let's dance," he says, pulling me up suddenly. "I like this song."

"Me, too!" cries Beth Ann. From the darkness she re-appears and thrusts her half-eaten hot dog into my hands.

"We may dance all night. You don't have to wait around for me," Beth Ann squeaks in my ear.

Suddenly I have had just about enough. "Actually, I will wait," I tell her, narrowing my eyes. Her own widen, and I know she doesn't understand, but I don't care. I am tired of being nice. As I watch them dance, the anger inside me grows. Beth Ann has her arms wrapped tight around Sully's middle, so tight the kid can barely breathe. She's also shorter than he is, a lot shorter, and so she stands on his feet as they sway back and forth. People are pointing, but Sully doesn't seem to mind.

"Well, that's a sight," Jade Winslow says as she plops herself next to me on the log. Before any other meanness can pop out of her perfectly pouty mouth, I stomp across the sand to where Beth Ann is suffocating Sully, and I tap her on the shoulder, hard.

"You know, Sully, I think I'd like that dance now."

Beth Ann barely has time to sputter before I step in.

"Thanks, Beth Ann," Sully tells her. But she doesn't go. She just stands there as I take her place, although I don't step on Sully's feet like she did. Everyone knows better than that.

Beth Ann is still standing behind me, her mouth open wide, as I wrap my arms around Sully's neck. I rest my head carefully on his shoulder and we dance. I don't know if Beth Ann is there or not, for it takes all my strength to stand on my shaking legs. Sully hums a little in my ear to the music, and without warning the tears start. They spill down my cheeks and onto his shirt, but still I hold on tight.

When the song ends, Sully leans back and inspects my face. "It's gonna be okay, Lace."

I nod, and he kisses me quickly on the forehead. Just once, real gentle. I suck in my breath. And, like Marni, he smells like sun and sand and grass. When he steps away and says good night, I turn back to the beach. Beth Ann is nowhere to be seen.

The Silent Treatment

Beth Ann will not speak to me. When I see her at the pool on Monday, I wave, but she disappears underwater and swims away. I know exactly what Beth Ann is doing and why. I was the worst. I had let her think Sully liked her. I butted in on their only dance, even if it was a stupid favor he was doing, even if he was just trying to be nice to her. I deserve to sit alone in the shade.

There is no reason for me to be at the pool now that Beth Ann is mad at me. I don't belong to the team, and I don't swim anymore. But still I show up with my suit in my bag and settle into a shady spot with my sketchbook. I can at least watch Beth Ann. And besides, Sully's smile reminds my heart to beat. By lunchtime on Tuesday, I am just about to leave when he comes over to me with his bologna sandwich in hand and hops onto the picnic table where I'm working on a picture.

"So what've you been up to?" Has he noticed that Beth Ann and I sit on opposite sides of the pool deck?

"Oh, this and that," I say, avoiding the truth that I sat home alone and watched TV for the past few nights.

"Well, I'm catching a movie tomorrow night if you'd like to join me," he offers casually.

Each Wednesday during the summer the local movie theater offers half-price tickets. Marni and I always used to go together. We could never agree on where to sit: she liked the front and I preferred the back. We disagreed on snacks, too. But once we were settled, somewhere in the middle of the theater with a small popcorn and a Hershey's bar between us, it was just us. The screen flickered, the lights went down, and we giggled conspiratorially in the dark. Even when her friends were there, it was me Marni always saved a seat for.

I haven't been to the movies all summer. A few feet away, Beth Ann dangles her feet in the pool. She looks over her shoulder with such sadness I know she's heard. Sully knows, too.

"You can bring a friend if you'd like."

"Okay," I tell him, my eyes on Beth Ann's skinny, freckled back. I want to yell, *Yes, yes, of course I will come to the movies with you.* I want to say, *No, she is not allowed to come with us.* But one look at her green goggles all crooked on her sad face and I just don't have it in me.

The Open Door

When I get home, the house is quiet. Halfway down the hall I see the open door. Anger rises inside me, and I storm toward it. How dare Willa Dodge go in Marni's room again? Dad told her that this room was off-limits. He told her not to go in there, not to tidy it up. I'll bet she's snooping around Marni's things. In my mind I think of the jeans tossed over her chair, the silver hairbrush left just so on her dresser. Was it angled left or right? Were her magazines at the head or the foot of her bed?

I am in a state by the time I reach her room, but what I see stops me at the door. It's not Willa Dodge. The room is dark and quiet, and a tall figure hunches on the bed hugging Marni's pillow. It's Dad. His back is to me, and he whimpers quietly as he moves. Back and forth, back and forth, he rocks. For all the times I've wanted to find him here, to know that he missed her, too, this is not how I thought it would feel.

Dad is always in control. I've been the one to stomp my feet, to get mad, to cry. I've been the one waking up with bad dreams. And I've been mad at him for staying so calm, so certain. It never occurred to me he wasn't.

Very quietly I pull the door closed, leaving Dad alone, alone with her things and his thoughts and his tears.

The Return

Early Wednesday morning the phone rings.

"Bean, how's my girl?" I'm so happy to hear Gran's voice, even if it is long distance.

"Are you still in Portland?" I ask.

"We're home," she tells me. "Got back last night. We thought we'd come see you, tell you all about it."

"Today?" I ask, crossing my fingers.

"Today," she says, laughing. "Grampa's got some important projects to finish in time for the homecoming. Plus, I was thinking we'd have us a little chat."

As promised, the red truck rattles into the driveway just before supper. I jump in the cab before Gran can undo her seat belt.

"My, what a welcome!" she laughs as we stumble out of the truck together.

"Make way, Trudy, it's my turn." Grampa whisks me up and spins me twice.

"How's my girl?" Gran asks, cupping my face in her hands. It feels like she's been gone for ages, after the last few days. Suddenly I'm so happy to have the Grands back. My eyes well up.

"I missed you," I manage to say. Gran studies me knowingly. I will tell her all about it later. And there are things she wants to tell me, I know. But for now we focus on our greeting.

"And how's our Willa?" Gran asks, smoothing her skirts from the long ride. I am surprised to hear Gran refer to her as "our" Willa. There is nothing about Willa Dodge that I want to be mine, or Gran's.

"Cooking," I say. "Kidney pie." I make a face,

expecting her to join in, but she raises her eyebrows thoughtfully. "That sounds good," she says, heading for the kitchen.

After the table has been set, I make a peanut butter sandwich and excuse myself before they sit down to Willa Dodge's pie. I want to hear about Portland, but I want to ask Gran in private. And there's the matter of Sully's movie invitation. It's Wednesday night.

"Aren't you eating with us?" Dad asks, eyeing my sandwich.

"Can't. I have a date," I inform them.

All heads turn.

"A what?" Dad yelps.

I have never been on a date. I have never even been asked out on a date, so I know this news is a shock.

But Gran rescues me. "A date? How wonderful! Go get yourself ready." She smiles at Dad, who looks back and forth from Gran to me.

Dad, always the team player, forces a weak smile.

"Go on," Gran says, shooing me away, and I make my escape.

Upstairs I grab the phone book off the hallway table and bring it to my room. *T, Ta, Tan, Tanner*, on *Dover Lane*. I dial the number fast, before I have time to change my mind. Sully picks up on the first ring, and I almost hang up.

"Uh, hi, Sully. It's Lace. I was just wondering if—"

"If I'm still up for the movie?" he asks.

"Yeah, the movie. If you still want to."

"Meet you there at seven?"

"Sure," I manage to squeak. The phone practically slides out of my sweaty hand into its base. I cannot believe I called Sully Tanner. I cannot believe he said yes.

Next I dial Beth Ann's number, but there is no answer. I leave a short message asking her to please call me. I don't mention the movie or Sully Tanner.

"In my day we wore dresses out on first dates." Gran smiles from the doorway at the mountain of blue jeans on my floor.

"It's not really a date, Gran," I tell her, but deep down I'm hoping it is.

"So, what are you wearing on this date?" she asks. Unlike Marni's closet, my own is T-shirts and shorts. Kid clothes. We settle on jeans and a cobalt blue shirt that matches my eyes.

"Now, let me get my hands on this hair!" Gran settles herself on the bed behind me. It's been a long time since Mom brushed my hair, and I almost melt against Gran.

"Gran?"

"Yes, Bean."

"What was it like?"

"Dating?"

"No. Portland."

The brush pauses in midair. "Well, I guess it was a lot of things. It was sad and sweet all mixed up together."

"What made you go?" I ask.

"I had to go. I had to see. These old eyes had to take it in so my heart could get used to it. As for your grampa, well, he just wanted to do. He's the doer of the family, as you know. So he got himself real busy out there, inspecting the place, making plans for the homecoming. There's a lot that needs to be changed back here. You'll see for yourself, when you go."

We sit on the bed real quiet, the *whoosh* of the brush through my hair the only sound in the room. "You and your sister have got your momma's hair. Like silk in the hand."

"Gran, what should I say when I see her?" I ask. The brush stops, and she rests her hand on my head.

"You don't need to do or say anything, Bean. You just got to get yourself there." Behind me, reflected in the mirror, Gran's eyes grow real soft as they look into my own. Here she is sending me all the love in the world. I sit up real straight and send it right back at her.

"Will you look at that," she says, and smiles. "So grown up, so beautiful like your sister."

Before following Gran downstairs, I stop outside Marni's room. It's chilly tonight, and I don't think she'd mind. Hanging on the hook inside her door is her navy swim team jacket, the *S.T.* for Saybrook Trout embroidered on the front. I pull it off and wrap it around my waist.

The Date

Sully Tanner is waiting inside the movie theater, leaning against the wall with a tub of popcorn.

"Hey there. Large popcorn, extra butter?"

"It's my favorite! How'd you know?"

"I just figured," he says quietly. The movie is already starting when we sit down. Sully passes the popcorn. Our elbows touch on the armrest, and shivers shoot up my neck. I hold my breath wondering if he'll put his arm around me. When he doesn't, I sink into my seat, leaning just a little in his direction for the rest of the movie.

Afterward we head out onto Main Street and make our way down to the coffeehouse. I recognize a crowd of teens gathered on the sidewalk in front, many wearing their swim team jackets as well. They wave to us, and Sully stops to greet them.

"I'm still kind of hungry," he says, looking in the window. "Want anything? Coffee? An ice cream?"

"Ice cream's great," I answer, happy that our evening isn't over yet.

When he heads into the shop, Jade Winslow sidles up to me, staring in her way that makes me feel very small. I pull

Marni's jacket around my shoulders and zip it up. Jade looks at it and smirks. She touches the letters *S.T.* on the front.

"Nice jacket," she sneers. She leans in closer and whispers, "You know, he's only being nice to you because he feels bad for you."

I look down at Marni's jacket in confusion. Before I can respond, Sully returns with two cones.

"Vanilla, right?" I smile real big for Jade, pleased that he remembered and that she is witness to it.

"Vanilla's perfect," I say.

Sully stops smiling and stares at me. I can feel the air shift.

"What is it?" I ask.

"Where'd you get that jacket?" He, too, is staring at my coat.

"It's Marni's. It's her swim team jacket. You must have one like it."

He looks uncomfortable.

"Yeah, I did." Sully listens to the chatter of the group around us but doesn't say anything. When they move off toward the park, a few of the guys invite him to come along. But Sully shakes his head and turns to me. "You know, Lace, I'm actually kind of tired. Maybe we should head home."

"Oh, okay," I stammer. My mind races. What just happened?

"Do you want me to walk you home?" he asks, shifting

uneasily from one foot to the other. I can tell he doesn't want to.

"No, thanks. I'll be fine." I try to read his expression, but he's staring at his sneakers.

"All right then, see you." He waves and walks briskly away, hands in his pockets, head down.

All the way home I replay the night in my head as vanilla ice cream runs down my hand. Sully was the one who asked me to the movie in the first place. Everything seemed fine. That is, until we ran into the swim team members. And what did Jade Winslow mean?

I throw the melted cone into the bushes outside our door. Let the chipmunks have it. I pass Dad watching TV in the den. The Grands are already in bed.

"So?" he asks eagerly, standing up. He's relieved to have me home, I can tell.

"It was fine," I mutter, taking the stairs two at a time. I don't want to talk to Dad right now.

In my room, Cinder thumps the bed happily with his tail. Before curling up next to him, I take off Marni's jacket and lay it carefully on my chair. It's then that I see the initials stitched across the front for what they are. *Sully Tanner.*

The Photo

In Marni's room, I stop at her bulletin board and stare at the many faces who love her and who she loves back. There is a photo of the whole family at Thanksgiving, both the wild-eyed Martins and the stern Wallaces. There's another photo of Marni hugging Cinder in the swaying hammock. Even Mom can't get him to jump into that hammock. But my favorite is the one of her and the team, arms thrown around each other, grinning widely on the dock. They're so close all you can see are faces. Marni glows, her wet hair slicked back, perfect white teeth popping against her tanned skin. Her girlfriends are crowded around, and Marni is perfectly in the middle. It's as if all the hugging arms are reaching to the center, to her. A couple of the boys frame the laughing group. It's then I notice one face not looking at the camera. I recognize the blond hair. It's Sully Tanner, looking past the others, face turned and eyes gazing at something in the center. At Marni.

Secrets

I never liked the dark. Ever since I can remember I have worried about the shadowy figures that roll past my window or down the hall at night. Lake monsters tapping at the glass, house monsters hovering in my doorway. As a little kid, I was certain there was something waiting to get me. I think that's how it started.

Marni was never afraid of these things, or if she was she didn't say so. Instead, she would sit up in bed when I appeared at her door and whisper calmly, "What's the matter?" I was probably four and she six when our nighttime visits began. At first, she used to tell me to go back to bed, reassuring me with the sleep-filled huskiness of her voice. But I wouldn't.

So after a few nights Marni conceded, and before I was even at her door her covers would be rolled back neatly on one side of the bed. At first we'd just go to sleep, me tucked quietly behind her, clutching my stuffed blue dog. Mom would find us in the morning and shake her head with a smile. She probably thought we'd outgrow it. But as we grew older, the visits continued. There were things to talk about. Like whether Mrs. Wifflin, my second-grade teacher, really had a mustache. And which set of monkey bars on the playground was the hardest. I didn't believe in monsters anymore by that time, but our nighttime visits were part of us, as much a part of our nightly rhythm as having breakfast was a part of each day. Sometimes Marni was wide-awake and lively, leaping around the room as she reenacted the fifth-grade food fight in the cafeteria. Other times she was thoughtful and quiet, wondering aloud, "Who do you think feeds the cats in Heaven?" when our old calico, Clara, died. Once, she curled herself around me while I cried over losing the fourth-grade spelling bee to Nancy Hardwick.

When Marni went to high school, I stopped going to her room at night. We had outgrown it, just as we'd outgrown squeezing into her single bed. But there were occasions when she began to come to mine. Marni got nervous the nights before her swim meets. She never said so, never complained about her times or worried out loud about the competition. But before a big meet she'd appear at my door, her long hair framing her pale face in the dark, pillow in hand. And I'd move over, throwing back the covers and inviting her in. We didn't talk then. She just lay beside me in the dark, her heart pounding under our shared blanket. Sometimes she'd reach for my hand and hold it. Soon her chest would rise and fall more slowly, her breath evening out. And then she'd sleep.

I remember the last time Marni came to my room. It

was just as school was letting out this summer. And it wasn't the night before a swim meet. She knocked quietly at my door and tiptoed to my bed's edge. "Lace?" she said, too loudly.

"What?" I mumbled, rousing reluctantly from a deep dream.

She snuggled in beside me, and I could sense her giddiness, the energy she'd brought to my sleepy room.

"Marni," I complained, rolling away and pulling the blanket over my head. "I'm tired." I had a social studies test the next day, one I wasn't prepared for. It was graduation week. I was exhausted from the end-of-school events and still undecided about what dress to wear under my cap and gown for my eighth-grade graduation. And Marni hadn't been around much herself. It seemed she was always going off somewhere with her friends. Talking on the phone late at night, or on the computer e-mailing.

I wasn't in the mood.

"I have a secret," she giggled, poking me in my side.

But I must have fallen asleep, because she never did tell me what it was. In fact, I'd forgotten completely that she'd tried.

Alone

The next day I stay home from the pool. Beth Ann still does not call or come by, and neither does Sully Tanner. I feel more alone than ever. I sit at the kitchen table, working on a portrait of Gran.

"Where'd that fine redheaded friend of yours get off to?" Grampa asks.

"She's around," I say, grabbing a red pencil. I work on the spoon in Gran's hand, smoothing the fingers wrapped confidently around its wooden handle.

"What about your date?" Gran whispers in my ear, placing a cookie on my page.

"It wasn't really a date," I tell her, taking a big bite.

"Oh?" she asks. Gran loves nothing more than a good story, and she can tell this is not how the story ended.

"I don't want to talk about it," I say, wiping the crumbs from my lips.

"Well, you chew on that awhile," she says. Somehow I don't think she means the cookie.

———

By Saturday it's so hot we drape ourselves around the house, moving slowly through the rooms like syrup. Grampa slumps against the deck stairs with a lemonade,

Gran slips into the rocker beside him. Even Dad abandons his stuffy bedroom to join us outside, sleeves rolled up, leaning gratefully into the faint lake breeze. With no excuse to avoid it any longer, I abandon the sticky group on the porch.

"I'm going to the pool," I inform them. I run up to Marni's room and grab the jacket from the hook once more.

At one end of the pool is a weekend beginner class. Sully holds on to their hands as they kick, big splashes covering his face so I can't see it. But I can hear his laugh just fine. I imagine him coming over and laughing with me. No luck. I wait for him to see me and wave. He doesn't.

So, I scan the pool deck for Beth Ann. There are no green-goggled faces, no splashing, awkward swimmers. Did she stay home? Then I see her. At the far end of one of the lanes is a pigtailed head moving smoothly toward me. Stroke, stroke, breathe. Beth Ann Watts is doing the crawl! And she is not sinking, though she does choke a little here and there. My heart leaps. I jump out of my chair and yell her name before I remember. She turns and looks my way. So I wave. But Beth Ann does not wave back. Instead she pulls her green goggles over her eyes and paddles off.

When the beginner swim class ends, I walk to the shallow end and kneel by the pool.

"I think this is yours," I say, setting the swim team

jacket on the deck. The embroidered initials *S.T.* flash in the sunlight.

Sully looks up at me, surprised. "Lace, you don't have to give this back." He says it so nicely I can tell he's sorry.

"Isn't it yours?"

"Yeah," he says, and nods. "But I gave it to her."

To Marni, not to me. I feel so foolish. I just want him to take the jacket.

"I didn't know," I tell him. And then I run. I run through the parking lot and down the hill. I run down Pratt Street and past the beach. I don't stop running until I reach my bedroom door, and I fling myself on the bed. So that's how Sully Tanner knew who I was. Knew everything. Even the extra butter on my popcorn. That's why he was so nice to me. It was for her, all along. I bury my head in the pillows.

"Lace, is everything all right?" Dad asks quietly, tapping on my door.

"I'm fine," I cry.

"You don't sound fine."

"Well, I am," I cry louder.

A few minutes later there is another knock.

"I said I was fine!" I yell.

"Lace, there's someone here to see you." It's Gran. Her voice is so soft I feel the shame rise in my chest.

"Coming."

On the back porch is Sully Tanner. His hands are stuffed awkwardly in his pockets.

"I'm sorry," he says when I come out. "I thought you knew."

I don't know what to say to this. He is S.T. The *S.T.* penciled in the margins of Marni's notebooks. On the note she left us. On the team jacket. Suddenly the pieces swirl together so I can make out the whole picture. It has been there all along, my own reflection blurring its edges.

Sully leans against the railing, eyes searching my face for forgiveness I don't have the right to withhold. It's not his fault.

"How long?" I ask, finally, sitting down.

"What?"

"How long have you and Marni been together?"

"Oh. Just since the start of summer," he says, looking out over the lake. "But I liked her long before that."

"Everyone does," I answer.

He smiles at this.

"I thought the jacket was hers," I say. "I didn't realize you were S.T. I thought it meant Saybrook Trout."

He shrugs. "It doesn't matter," he says. "I gave it to her at the end of the school year. Just when we started going out."

"I can't believe she didn't tell me," I say.

"It was new to both of us," Sully replies. "Not exactly

a secret, but something we wanted to hold on to for ourselves I guess."

I have a secret, she'd whispered. She'd tried to tell me.

There is something else I need to know.

"Was it you?" I ask him. "Were you the one who went in after her?"

"I did," he says, closing his eyes tightly. "I pulled her out."

We'd known that kids had tried to find her, that people had dived in looking. But in all the chaos and the aftermath, no one had ever stepped forward to say who had reached her first. Who had grabbed her wrist underwater, pulled her from the murky depths. I was glad it was Sully. It was as it should have been.

The wind tickles the branches above us and they creak with soft laughter.

"Did you love her?" I ask.

Sully doesn't pause. "I still do," he whispers.

The sun is setting over the lake and the sky arches its back, orange and red tracing the horizon. Despite everything, it almost looks beautiful to me.

"How do you do it? How do you still go in?" I ask, nodding toward the water, thinking of him diving in at the meets, competing in the same water that took her away from us this summer.

Sully looks at me. "Simple. It's her favorite place. I feel

her out there." He turns away then. He rests his face in his hands, and soon his back begins to heave. Unlike my own, Sully's crying is soft.

"I miss her," he says.

He sinks on the bench beside me, and we sit, shoulder to shoulder, like two battered bookends holding up all the sadness in the world. This time I put my arm around him, and Cinder wedges under the bench beneath us, his black fur collecting our tears like gemstones.

The Midnight Search

I cannot sleep. If Beth Ann isn't going to help me with Willa Dodge, and my family won't listen, then I am on my own. My mind spins and teeters, all of what happened tonight swirling at a dizzying speed that leaves me slightly sick and wide-awake. Just before midnight there is the gentle pad of footsteps down the stairs, and the house goes quiet. I wait by the window, watching Willa move through the moonlit darkness and across the yard, stepping gingerly into the trees where I can no longer follow her. But I know she is at the lake. There is no point in going out. Tonight I need to focus on my time inside.

Outside Willa Dodge's closed door, I take a deep breath.

The handle turns easily in my sweaty hand. Inside, the room is neat as a pin. There are no clothes tossed on the armchair, no books on the bedside table. Even the bed itself is neatly made, clearly unslept in. Strange, I think. I move to the closet, pausing to listen for footsteps in the hall.

First, I stop at the dresser. I feel around each drawer, reaching under her clothing for clues. There's the usual: socks, shirts, a lumpy sweater in the bottom drawer. No watch, nothing of ours that shouldn't be there. I peer under the bed, and again I see the rolled map, but nothing else. I'm dying to turn on a light, but it would give me away if she happens to look back up at the house. So I tiptoe across the dimly lit room toward the closet. The doors creak open, and there in the corner is the suitcase. And even though I can't see, I know it's green. I pull it out slowly. It's a big bag. A big bag that could hold almost anything. The zipper hangs open like a gaping mouth, and from within something glimmers. Something silvery, something metal. I reach inside and hold my treasure up to the window for a better look. I recognize it right away. It's one of Marni's swim trophies. Inside the suitcase there are three more. Suddenly the empty shelf in Marni's room flashes back to me. I knew it! Willa Dodge is a thief after all. I've got to tell Dad.

But just then, from downstairs, comes the gentle slap of the screen door. She's back. Quickly I close up the suitcase and stuff it back in the closet. Only the doors won't close. A strap from the suitcase is jammed under the door. I tug at the strap, but it's really jammed under the door. My heart pounds. Willa's got to be at the bottom of the stairs by now. Desperate, I give the suitcase a final pull, and it yanks free. I slam the closet door shut and race for the door, back down the hall, and into my room. My heart is beating in my ears, but almost immediately there are the familiar steps on the stairs. They grow closer, pass my door, and disappear. I sink to the floor and wait. I want to show Dad the suitcase, but first I need to know more. Like why there's a map of our house under her bed. And why she'd want a teenage girl's trophies. I think of what Marni would do. She would be brave. She would unravel the whole story.

Sticking Up

By Monday I am determined to make things right with Beth Ann. But when I get to the pool, practice is about to start and the team is gathering poolside. A few of Marni's friends smile awkwardly, as usual. Alex and Jen wave at me, and I wave back, gratefully. Sully isn't among them, but Beth Ann is. I had hoped to talk to her in private.

"Oh, look, it's Lacey Martin." Jade Winslow is draped casually across a pool chair like she's on display. Swim team members crowd around her, bending close to chat. The whole group turns to me.

"Did you have fun at the movies the other night? It was so nice of Sully to babysit you like that."

"Lay off," Alex tells her, but Jade shrugs.

Jade's words sting, because I know there's some truth to what she says. Sully was only being nice to me. He was looking out for Marni's kid sister. He was doing it with Marni in mind.

Still, I try to ignore her, unfolding my towel on a lounge a few chairs away. I will not let her push me to the other end of the pool.

"We're going down to the lake for another bonfire tonight," Jade says, rising with the other swimmers and heading to the edge of the pool. She adjusts her pink cap neatly on her head and looks over her shoulder at me. "Sully and I will be going together, of course. Maybe you can tag along. That is, if Sully isn't tired of you following him around by then."

"Why do you have to be such a bully?" someone asks. It is a small voice, a voice I know well.

"Excuse me?" Jade asks, laughing.

"You heard me," Beth Ann says.

The swimmers part as a small, wiry figure plants herself right in front of Jade Winslow. Beth Ann stares at Jade through her magnified-vision water goggles. Her eyes are the size of soda bottle bottoms, large and glowing. And they are something else. Determined. This is not the Beth Ann I know.

"You're just jealous," Beth Ann continues. "You've always been jealous of Marni Martin."

The others look away. Beth Ann is right, and they know it.

Jade's face flushes red, her mouth tight. "That's ridiculous," she sputters.

"No, it's not," Beth Ann says. "You probably figured you'd take her place now, but you can't. Your swim times rot, your stroke is sloppy. And to top it off, you're a big, fat meanie."

"You little brat," Jade hisses, placing her hands on her hips. "You're a joke in the pool. Get out of my way."

But Beth Ann doesn't move.

I sit, glued to my lounge chair. I cannot believe what Beth Ann is saying. "You can't stand it. Lace's sister was a better swimmer than you. And more popular than you. And nicer than you. Everyone still thinks so. And best of all, Sully Tanner does, too!"

With that Beth Ann jumps into the pool, paddling and kicking furiously down the lane, her giant green flippers rising out of the water and splashing Jade from head to toe. Sputtering and gasping, Jade jumps back.

A whistle blows, and we all look over at Sully Tanner. "What's going on?" he asks.

"Nothing!" Jade shrieks, heading for her chair and grabbing her towel. She storms off the pool deck.

I swipe the wet hair from my face and look over at Beth Ann.

"Thanks," I mouth, but she's already underwater, moving down her lane.

The Winner Is . . .

When the sound of footsteps echoes down the hall, I roll out of my bed. Willa Dodge is outside. The whole house is quiet, sighing now and then under the weight of family sleep.

In her room, I hurry to the closet and yank the green suitcase out with one fierce pull. When I unzip it, the contents shimmer from within. There, lying like fallen soldiers, Marni's trophies gleam. There are four in all, and the whole bag glows like an opened chest of treasure.

Why would Willa Dodge steal them? The pounding of fear in my heart gives way to the pounding of anger. Marni worked hard for these trophies! Gently I pull the trophies from the suitcase, one by one. Willa will come back and find them gone. She will probably even know it was I who took them. But I don't care. By then I will have told Dad, and he'll be waiting with me for her return. He'll finally see what I have been trying to show him.

Together we'll confront her in the hall, and she will be fired on the spot. She will have to pack her bags and leave in the middle of the night.

The trophies are heavier than I expected, so I carry two at a time back to Marni's room. The sweet smell of summer meets me when I open the door, and I hurry in with my load of treasure. I place each trophy carefully in front of her dresser mirror. In the reflection it looks like there are eight. Good, I think. Marni would be proud of me.

As I slide the last one into position, I notice the engraved plate on the trophy base. The year is 1967.

That isn't right. Marni won these just last year. We weren't even born in 1967. I grab the trophy and hurry to the window, where the light is stronger. There in the moonlight I can read the entire inscription: 1967 100-METER BUTTERFLY.

And then I see the name. WILLAMINA DODGE.

Into the Fog

Outside, the air is damp and cool and still. Willa Dodge is nowhere in sight, so I sit on the steps until I get my bearings. It's eerie how silent a busy town can be at night. No cars, no birds, no beachgoers. It's as if Willa Dodge and I are the only two people on earth. Cautiously, I step down the porch stairs into the damp yard and make my way across it. I pass Mom's garden beds, her silvery shrubs dappled with moonlight. Beyond the garden, Willa has long since disappeared into the mist. As I crest the edge of the yard where the grass slopes to the water, the smell of the lake fills my head, but I stay the course, making my way carefully down the rocky path to the beach. To the lake.

Quietly, I follow Willa Dodge, careful to conceal myself as I approach her. Above, the moon is full-faced, suspended over the water. It outlines Willa Dodge's figure on the shore ahead of me, softening her shape as she stretches on the sand. I settle myself behind a fallen tree. Beneath me the cool sand cups my knees.

At the shore Willa Dodge bends to touch the water, a long, flat object in her other hand. And then she turns. I shudder, pressing myself as flat as possible into the sand. All four trophies said the same thing: WILLAMINA DODGE. What will I say if she finds me? But she does not turn in my direction. Instead she bends, holding the objects in her hands to her feet. I realize they are flippers. The very things she must have been removing and replacing in the green suitcase each night. The *whoosh* of the zipper echoes in my mind, and I cringe, feeling ridiculous.

Into the water she moves steadily, almost graceful. The water parts in pale waves. A breeze stirs, and it sounds like the lake is sighing. Her upper body slips beneath the dark surface, a glowing halo of moonlight rippling around her. It's hard to tell where Willa stops and the lake begins. Her strokes are effortless and clean, the strokes of a seasoned swimmer, someone at ease in the water. I am caught off guard by all of this. By the sad-eyed moon and the smell of the lake rising in my chest, by the woman moving silently through the water. Shame fills my little hiding spot behind the tree. I am a spy. And Willa Dodge is just a swimmer. A trophy-winning swimmer who brought her memories with her in a green suitcase. Stealing away from our house, from our sadness, and our troubles.

I remember what Grampa Martin said, of swiping at things when we are mad. Of the crazy notions a person gets. And of fixing things that are really broken, and leaving alone those that are not. Fog rises off the water as Willa moves out into the lake. With each gentle stroke, Willa Dodge glides away from the shore. Away from me and my crazy notions, a glimmering veil of moonlight trailing in her wake.

The Trip

I don't do well on long car trips. I have to sit in the front seat so I don't get sick. If I try to read a book, the nausea overwhelms me by the second page. Mom calls it motion sickness. Dad says it's a good thing we don't live on a boat.

But on this trip, the nausea starts even before Dad turns on the ignition.

"You'll be fine," the Grands told me as we packed the car. Gran set a little tin of ginger cookies on the seat beside me, and Grampa handed me a small rectangular box. "Save it for the road," he said with a wink. I placed them both alongside a small package, wrapped in tissue, that Sully had brought by the house just the night before. He'd knocked on the door after dinner.

"I heard you're going," he'd said, his voice serious.

When I'd nodded, he'd pulled the package from the crook of his arm, handing it over with a gentleness I imagined people use to pass new babies. He didn't need to say any more. I accepted it carefully, and our eyes met.

"I'll take care of it," I'd promised.

Now, Dad and I head south, down the interstate, mile after mile passing in a haze outside the car window. I don't see the tiny towns we sail past, the tourists lining the rest-stop exit ramps. I try to eat when Dad passes me a sandwich, try to nod at the small conversation he attempts to make. But my mind is already miles ahead, beyond the asphalt that hums warily beneath our tires.

Halfway to Portland, Dad pulls into a rest stop for gas, and we both get out of the car to stretch our legs. At a picnic table in the shade, I open the box Grampa has given me. A wooden frame slides out in my hand, and I turn it over to examine the picture behind the glass. It's a black-and-white photo, of Marni and me, taken last summer. We're sitting on the dock in our swimsuits, back to back, our arms wrapped around our knees, smiling at the camera like mirror images of one another. Our hair is sleek and wet, probably fresh out of the lake. For the first time I realize how much alike we look. The matching wide smiles, the freckled noses. In this photo we are sisters, bound by the blood that courses through our veins just as we are bound by the lake that looms beneath us.

When Dad calls me, I hurry back to the car. With each passing exit, my fingers grip the edge of my seat a little harder, and I close my eyes against the dull afternoon sun that presses ominously on our little car and the small treasures it holds.

The Reunion

Mom is waiting for us when we pull into the parking lot of her apartment, I can feel it. I have barely undone my seat belt when she is there, beside my door, struggling with the handle.

"Lacey," she cries, pulling me to her like a riptide, my arms and legs and head all swept into her at once. Fiercer than one of Grampa Martin's bear hugs.

"You're finally here," she says, holding me out to get a

good look. And she does. She looks at me hard, her eyes smiling and full of tears at the same time.

I want to smile back, but suddenly my knees start to shake and I just can't hold myself up or hold myself in anymore. My legs crumple, and I fall right into her arms and cry like a little baby.

"What? What, honey?" Mom's voice is worried. She clutches me tight and rocks me against her. "Shh, shh, Lacey. I'm here, honey, I've got you."

I realize for the first time how unnatural it's been to be without Mom this summer. I've worked so hard not to think about all that has happened, and it is the hardest work I've ever done. In not thinking about that day, I've had to not think about Mom and Marni. But now, tucked into her arms, her curly hair falling around my face, her voice in my ear, I just give up. She is as much in me as my very bones are. And I am glad of that. Now everything feels the same for a minute, and my chest aches with the fullness of it all.

But Mom is different. She looks tired, and the corners of her eyes don't crinkle when she smiles.

Standing in the middle of a parking lot in this strange new apartment complex, I know it's never going to be the same again. The tears come until my body shudders with the realization of it all.

"Are we ready?" Dad asks, coming around the car

with our bags. He has a feverish look about him, an urgency in his gait.

Mom shakes her head and squeezes his arm. "I think you should go alone," she tells him, wrapping her arm around me. "It's too much right now. Lace and I'll make some dinner and go in the morning." She looks at me, gently sweeping the hair back from my forehead, and I nod gratefully, sinking against her.

"Of course," Dad agrees, resting his hand on my head. "I'll call you in a little while."

There is the exchanging of bags and of words that carry important information. I tuck the package from Sully into my backpack. Dad hugs Mom fiercely and kisses me on the forehead before he climbs back into our car. "It's going to be okay," he says, leaning out the window. "I'll see you in the morning." And then he drives away.

"Let's go inside and get you settled," Mom says, picking up my duffel bag and reaching for my hand. "You must be tired."

The apartment is tiny, a little bedroom and a kitchen, all in one space. It feels weird, being in this place that Mom has lived in without us. This is not home. The bathroom is so small Cinder couldn't turn around in it.

"It's not home," Mom says as if reading my thoughts and laughs uneasily as she makes dinner. "But it's close to the hospital." We sit and eat supper like she's never been gone, like we've not missed a single meal together.

Afterward we climb together into the tiny bed, where Mom wraps the blanket around us.

"Tell me," she whispers, snuggling close. "Tell me about Daddy, and the Grands, and you. I want to hear it all."

So I do. I tell her about Dad's work and the Grands' visits, about the cook-off and Beth Ann's swimming lessons, and even about Willa Dodge. And the more I talk, the more the tiredness lifts from her face, and the corners of her eyes crinkle again with happiness in the dark.

I leave out two things. I don't tell her about the green suitcase and my crazy notions. I can't admit that I was a spy. The other thing I do not mention is Sully Tanner.

"What a summer," she says with a sigh when I'm done. "And that Willa! Does Cinder really let her give him baths?"

I nod in the dim light.

"Marvelous."

And then the crazy notions fill my head again. What if Mom thinks we don't need her anymore? What if she doesn't come home? But before I can ask, her breathing grows slow and deep, her hug heavier. And so I wait for sleep to find me, in the tiny bed in the tiny apartment, Mom murmuring in my ear while tomorrow roars outside our window.

Then

That night I dream. I dream of Turtle Rock and the afternoon of the accident. The air is thick and hot and slow, like honey, and just about everyone presses into the lake seeking relief. Beth Ann and I are playing tag on the beach with some of the younger kids, and it's not really fair because she's wearing her father's underwater X-ray vision goggles and therefore she's blind as a bat. I could stand still and she'd unknowingly run past me.

Marni has just arrived at the beach with a bunch of friends and is splashing around with them. She joins me on the sand after a quick swim. "We're going to the cove to jump off Turtle Rock, want to come?"

Beth Ann runs past us, grasping at the air. "You're it," she yells, slapping an elderly man on the back.

"Over here, Beth Ann!" Marni and I shout, giggling hysterically.

"Who's going?" I ask.

Marni wraps her towel loosely around her narrow waist. "Some kids from the team. You should come."

Beth Ann joins us, having finally removed her goggles. "Let's go!" she says, excited at the idea of an afternoon with Marni and her friends.

Some of the swimmers pass us, grinning. A few of the boys glance at her shyly, some smiling over their shoulder. "See you at the cove!" one shouts, adding playfully, "No little sisters allowed!"

I narrow my eyes at them. Marni, unaware of the attention as usual, wrings the water from her long hair and sweeps it behind her.

"So, are you coming?" she asks hopefully.

"Nah, I'd rather stay here," I say. Suddenly I am tired of being her little sister. I am tired of watching everyone watch her.

"I want to jump off Turtle Rock," she adds. "Come with me!"

My stomach turns. Marni knows I am afraid to jump off Turtle Rock, and yet each time they go she begs me to jump with her. I don't think Marni has ever been afraid of anything.

"Come on," Beth Ann pleads, eager to be part of the group.

"Oh, all right," I agree reluctantly, trudging after my sister.

Marni's friends Jennifer and Alex are waiting in the parking lot. We meet up with them and cross the pavement. The group thins out into a line as we hit the dirt path that winds along the road. It's hot, and Beth Ann huffs noisily behind me.

"Do you think she'll jump?" she asks. "It's so high!"

I ignore her, wondering if Marni really will. Wondering if I can.

We continue along the road, the group growing louder as we near the cove. Turtle Rock is the highest ledge along the lake. To get to it, we follow the well-worn path away from the road, up into a patch of scrubby trees and grass. You can see the shimmer through the branches as we make our way out toward the ledge, among the rocks. The trees thin, and suddenly we're at a rock clearing directly over the water. Below us, around the bend, is the beach we just came from. The view is sharp and clear, the body of dark green water below foreboding. The boys lurch ahead, Sully Tanner among them, dropping towels, vying for positions near the rock face. Marni and her friends join them, peering over the edge.

"Come on," Marni calls, waving to me over her shoulder.

I inch toward the edge, eyeing my feet on the rock cropping, wary of their placement.

Marni shakes her head and laughs. "Closer!" she teases.

Ahead of us the first of three boys peels off his T-shirt and whirls it around his head. "Bombs away!" he shouts.

The group cheers, and he launches himself feetfirst, cannonball style, over the edge. There is a loud splash twenty feet below, and a hush falls over the group as he disappears beneath the surface. I swallow hard, stepping away from the edge. And then he bursts to the surface and everyone cheers. Next, Sully takes his position at the ledge, grins once over his shoulder at us, and jumps. Everyone hoots again.

"You game?" Marni asks, grabbing my hand and squeezing it as the next boy jumps.

I look warily at her.

"I'm not going," Jennifer says, shaking her head emphatically. "No way!"

"Maybe next time," agrees Alex, settling herself on a rock far away from the ledge.

"That leaves us," Marni says, her eyes crinkling with excitement. She's never jumped before. She's always wanted to. And she's always wanted me to jump with her.

"You're really going to do it?" Beth Ann asks me. She looks worried and impressed all at once.

Jade Winslow joins our group, kicking off her flip-flops purposefully. "I am," she announces, raising her chin.

"We are, too," Marni tells her.

I look hard at Marni. I know how important this is to her. She must've asked me a hundred times last summer. She wouldn't ask me to do something she didn't think was safe.

There is a sudden crashing in the bushes and undergrowth behind us. Sully and the other boys scramble back up the trail, wet and heady with the thrill.

"That was great!" he shouts, joining us. There is a flurry

of high-fiving, the good-natured slapping of hands on wet backs. Everyone's whooping like warriors as another kid jumps. Jade Winslow, who still hasn't gone, is beaming at the boys instead. There is a pulse on the rock, and, suddenly, I feel a part of it. And it feels good.

"Who's next?" Sully shouts.

"We are!" I shout back.

I'm just as surprised as Beth Ann, who yelps, "Are you crazy?"

"She's my girl!" Marni cheers. She tugs my hand toward the ledge, grinning the whole way. The crowd steps back, patting us on the back, cheering us on, and suddenly we're alone at the edge. Marni looks at me. "It's just us, weasel."

I stand frozen in place, squeezing her hand. It's cold, the wind rising up over the water. My stomach drops when I look down. It's our turn, but I am not ready. I look out at the horizon and try to take a deep breath, but my lungs refuse to fill and the breath escapes my chest in a frenzied wheeze.

"You all right?" Marni asks.

I nod, but I want to shake my head no.

"Get on with it," calls Jade Winslow.

"Be careful!" whines Beth Ann from somewhere behind us.

"Ready?" Marni asks, bending her knees.

I look down again and realize I cannot do this.

"I can't," I whisper, stepping back.

Marni looks at me. "You can!" she says.

But the contagious excitement from before has left me, the throbbing pulse silenced. I shake my head no.

Marni sighs with her whole body and steps away with me. She is disappointed but doesn't say so.

Beth Ann hurries up beside me and pats my arm sympathetically. Jade Winslow smirks as we pass her.

"Bawk, bawk, bawk," squawks one of the boys, taking our place on the ledge. My face goes red.

Marni tosses him a mean look. "Just give her a minute," she says. "She'll change her mind."

But I can't.

"I said no," I snap. I have no reason to be mad at Marni, but I am. Suddenly I am furious. With her, and the crowd around her. And myself. I grab my towel and hurry toward the path. Beth Ann scrambles after me.

"Wait!" Marni calls, catching up with us. "Ignore them," she tells me. "It's no big deal."

But it is. Sully trots up behind us. "Hey, Marni, you can jump with us if you want," he says, touching her arm lightly.

She considers this, looking at me.

"Sullyyyy!" someone shouts from below. "You guys coming?"

He looks impatiently over his shoulder.

"I'll come," Marni tells Sully, her mind made up. And even though this is her jump, and we both know she is the one who wanted us to do this together, I am filled with a rush of betrayal. Marni is not afraid. And her friends are waiting for her to jump.

"Want to watch?" she asks me as she starts back up the trail behind Sully.

I do not want to watch. I am tired of being the watcher.

"Just go," I snap at her. "Your fans are waiting."

Her eyes widen, but before Marni can say anything, her friends start calling to her, telling her to hurry up. She turns away, leaving me to stew in my own meanness.

"Show-off!" I shout after her. But she's already gone.

Beth Ann gives me a look, but I'm already ashamed. I kick a stray rock and clamber down the path without looking back.

"Let's go to the beach," I mutter. So we do.

We hike along the road, silent on our trek, until we reach the sand. The farther we get from Turtle Rock the easier I can breathe. We get an ice cream from the truck in the parking lot and find a good spot on the sand to lay our towels. It's hard not to think about the kids back at Turtle Rock, but after an hour I imagine they've left anyway. Beth Ann talks and talks about nothing in particular, and I stretch out on my towel, soaking up the last of the late afternoon sun. I'm starting to feel a little better when I hear the sirens.

At first there is a gentle wail, like a strong lake breeze. But it grows. Soon people rise from their beach chairs and shade their eyes, looking in its direction.

"What's going on?" Beth Ann asks worriedly. As the sirens pierce the beach, an ambulance roars past on the road. A police car follows, and then another. They don't pull into the beach lot but drive right by it, parking on the lake road below our house. By the cove.

"Oh no, I hope someone isn't hurt!" Beth Ann says.

As if in response, Jennifer trots across the parking lot, flapping her hands and crying. She stops at a group of other kids. "There's been an accident at Turtle Rock!" she cries.

And I know.

I lurch forward, toward the sirens, my own lungs wailing in my chest. The heat presses against me, wraps itself around me, and I run until I think I will burst. When I reach the porch steps, I am flailing, grasping at the rail to pull myself up. The house is oddly quiet as I surge inside.

"Where is she?" I yell. "Is she home?"

Mom has just come in the door, car keys in hand. "Who?" she asks, setting down a bag of groceries on the kitchen counter.

Dad comes downstairs. "What's going on out there?" he asks, peering out the window.

And before I can answer there is the knock on the front door. The knock that rings through the house, that will ring through our memories for the rest of our lives. And as the policeman sits my parents down, as Mom cries out and Dad runs to the door, I tuck the note Marni left on the kitchen counter in my pocket. Then I go to my room, where I lie on the floor until they come to tell me what I already know.

Now

Mom and I get up early the next morning and hop in the rental car. In less than five minutes we pull up to the Portland Rehabilitation Hospital.

"This is it," she says. Hospitals scare me. There is that smell of disinfectant mixed with the stale smell of sickness. It makes me think of needles and operating tables and really old people with tubes coming out of their bodies in every direction. Dad calls it the smell of fear.

When we enter the lobby and take the elevator to the third floor, I don't smell any of these things. This hospital feels different. There are kids and grownups in the hall. We pass large open rooms filled with gym equipment. There are mirrors on the walls and mats on the floor and railings and ramps and bars. It looks a little like our school gymnasium when the teacher sets up the gymnastics course each winter.

Mom squeezes my hand. As we make our way down

the corridor, I notice something else. This hallway is lined with wheelchairs.

Outside Room 27 we stop. The door is cracked so that just a little sunlight streams through, splashing the toes of my red sneakers.

Mom smiles. "You ready?"

I don't think I will ever be ready to open this door. How can I want so bad to be on the other side and still want to run past it at the same time? My stomach rises into my throat. Mom puts on a big smile and pushes the door open.

"Good morning, sunshine. Look who I brought with me."

The Truth

The room is flooded with morning light. And it is strangely so familiar. There is a rocking chair draped with one of Gran's patchwork quilts. Dad waves at me from where he stands beside the dresser, a dresser covered with framed faces smiling out at me: Mom, Dad, Cinder, even my own welcome me. The wall is covered with greeting cards and posters. There are sports magazines on a bedside stand. And there is the pale girl in the bed, chestnut hair spilling onto white pillows, a fallen little bird. She blinks at us.

"Lace!" Marni's voice is almost her own. Ragged, but

crisp with laughter around the edges. She struggles to sit up, holding the edge of the bed, pulling herself upright. It takes all her effort, and Mom rushes forward to help.

"I got it," Marni says, holding her hand up to stop her.

Mom and Dad embrace and watch, wiping at their eyes.

Marni frowns at them both. "See?" She grins weakly, sinking against the pillow. Her eyes look larger against the hollowness of her face. "Get over here, weasel," she says.

As I hug Marni's bony back, I bury my face in her hair. It's a relief. Even here she smells like sun and sand and grass.

A nurse comes in with breakfast.

"Can't say I recommend the food, but the service is great," Marni says, winking at the nurse. She takes a small bite and grimaces. "Five stars." She coughs. That's Marni for you. Here she is trying to make me laugh, to make me comfortable.

Mom and Dad stay awhile, talking for us and around us. There is a visit from the doctor, nurses' rounds. All of it busy and bustling, and I watch as Marni tires from it. Her speech slurs, just a little, from time to time. Mom told me that this was a normal part of recovery, and that the doctors had assured her it was improving quickly. Mom motions for me to come sit with them by the window, to give Marni a break. And in no time she is sleeping, her expression peaceful and smooth against the white pillow.

Mom and Dad step into the hall to talk with a specialist, and I sit quietly by her bed, watching. I watch her all morning, as nurses come in and out, as she rouses for a sip of water, and slips back into sleep. She is so small.

Later, as the sun makes its way across the sky, Marni awakens with more strength and wants to talk. I help her spread the photos I've brought across the bed. She is hungry for information. "What's everyone *doing*?" she keeps asking. Sometimes Marni forgets things, and sometimes she asks me a question I've already answered. Mom warned me this might happen. And though it doesn't bother me, I can tell it upsets Marni. So, when she gets quiet and crosses her arms, I tell her again. I tell Marni about Cinder and Dad, about Beth Ann's father's latest inventions. I tell her I went to the bonfire. I decide not to tell her anything having to do with the pool or the lake. But she isn't satisfied.

"What else?" she begs. So I talk about Gran and Grampa, and describe Willa Dodge. I even tell her how Beth Ann and I aren't talking, though I don't say exactly why. This news is more interesting, and it quiets her for a while. But soon she wants more.

"What about the team?" she asks finally. "How's their season going?"

Mom told me they have made it a point not to talk about the team, or the lake. They didn't want to upset her.

I look to her for help now, but she just shrugs. So I give Marni the scores. They upset her.

"I can't believe they won't make it to finals this year."

I want to tell her it's because she wasn't there, but I stop myself. Suddenly it seems like there is nothing we can talk about without including the lake, or why she's been away from it. Or the fact that her two skinny legs hidden under the sheets do not work anymore. And may not ever work again, here or at home, on the land or in the water. The lake and the accident are everywhere, and there's no escape.

But then a wheelchair rolls through the door. "Your chariot, my lady!" A young man appears behind it, grinning widely. This pleases Marni, who giggles and pulls herself up. His name tag says "Johnny," and he is her physical therapist. He's young and handsome, and there is a flurry of activity as he lowers her bed and adjusts the bars for her. "Want to take a spin?" he asks.

Mom moves out of the way and busies herself with the breakfast tray. But I can't take my eyes off Marni. Johnny throws back the bedsheet to reveal Marni's coltish, folded legs. Her strong, muscled limbs have wilted, shrunken in their quiet. It's like part of her is missing.

"Ready?" Johnny asks. Marni wraps her arms around his neck, draping herself against him. Carefully he lifts her up and off the bed, pivoting toward the wheelchair.

"Nice and easy," he encourages. Marni's upper body arches in effort, but her lower body sways beneath her, trailing like a pale gown. I turn away, studying the parking lot from the window, until they roll down the hall followed by my dad.

Mom grabs my hand and turns me around. "Are you all right?"

"Yeah," I say. "Just tired, I guess." It's then I notice the trophies. All four of Marni's trophies are lined up, proud and tall on a table by the door. I walk to the table and grab one.

"How did these get here?" I ask my mom.

"Those? Oh, they were sent out here a couple of weeks ago."

"Did Marni ask for them?"

"No, that's the thing. They were just delivered to her room one afternoon. At first I worried they'd upset her. But she was thrilled. I think they cheer her on. Remind her of home."

I finger the nameplate. MARNI MARTIN. 100-METER BUTTERFLY. "It was nice of Daddy to send them."

"Daddy didn't send them. He was as surprised as I was when I told him."

"Then who did?"

"Willa Dodge. It was her idea."

Therapy

"Come on," Mom calls from the hall. "You won't believe how far she's come."

But Mom forgets that this is new to me. I still can't believe how far she's fallen.

Marni is already positioned on a set of parallel bars in the small gym. Johnny spots her from behind, a look of concentration furrowing his brow.

"Let's see how far we get today. Remember, envision what it is you want your body to do. Power it down into your legs."

Marni's arms shake, bearing her weight. Slowly, one hand at a time, she moves herself along between the bars. I hold my breath. Beneath her, her legs dangle, dragging when they touch the ground until she pulls herself up again, groaning in effort. If they move at all, I cannot tell. To me they are lifeless.

"Isn't it wonderful?" Mom asks. Her face is lit up. But I feel sick.

"Wonderful?" I whisper. "She can't walk." The tears start by themselves, and it's too late.

Mom grabs my arms and pulls me into the hall, looking both angry and sorry. "Don't ever let Marni hear that!"

she whispers fiercely. Her face is inches away, red with disappointment. "Do you know how hard she's worked? None of these doctors can guarantee anything, but we know Marni. We know her, Lace, and if anyone can do it, she can. Right?" Mom looks ready to break.

"Right," I whimper as she wraps her arms around me. I have no right to cry for myself. "I'm sorry," I say, wiping my face.

Mom sighs. "You're right, too, honey, this is awful. It's the most awful, unfair thing. But we have to be strong for her, you understand?"

We return to the gym, where Marni groans at the bars, her face sweating with effort. When she is done, Mom and Dad wheel her back to her room full of praise and encouragement.

Johnny makes notes on her chart. "So, you're the sister. Are you a swimmer, too?" he asks.

"None of us swim anymore," I say.

He puts her chart down. "That's too bad. I hear you're both pretty good," he says.

"She was a champion," I tell him.

Johnny closes her file and looks at me. "She still is," he says.

Rehab

I spend the rest of the week with Marni at the rehab hospital. I watch from the sidelines as she works at her therapy, a different workout than I am accustomed to her doing, but the hardest workout I have ever witnessed her endure. Johnny is right, she is still a champion.

Her days are scheduled, one therapy session after another. Each morning she is visited by the hospital's speech pathologist. Her name is Dawn, and she is young and enthusiastic. She sits with Marni, taking her through articulation exercises. Marni's speech is much better, but she starts to slur a little when she gets tired. Mom says her facial muscles are still weak.

Afterward, Marni goes to the therapeutic recreation class, where she joins other patients at a long table. Aside from the wheelchairs and walkers, it is not unlike the art room at our old scout camp, where we sat on picnic benches and strung lanyards or worked on misshapen clay pots that Mom would exclaim over when we returned home after our two-week stay. Marni was impatient with arts and crafts even then; now her dark brows furrow in concentration as she struggles with a paintbrush.

But the hardest part of her day is to come. After lunch

is her physical therapy in the hospital pool. I watch through the window as they seat her on the hydraulic lift at the pool's edge. The lift is large. And it steals my breath away. I touch my chest, watching Marni being lowered into the water by this chrome contraption. There is no roaring crowd, no competition in the lane beside her. Suddenly the smell of chlorine makes me weak with nausea, but I don't leave her this time. When she looks over at us, I give her the thumbs-up, swiping quickly at a stray tear that's dared to escape.

By Saturday, I am exhausted, and I can see she is, too. But the therapists and doctors marvel at her progress, assuring Mom and Dad that her age and her health have allowed her a remarkable recovery. We are lucky, they say. Her coma was brief, only twelve hours. The hemiparesis she suffered from the blow to her head has impaired the left side of her body. But she will walk again, if imbalanced. She may never recover the full strength of the left side of her body. She will need a cane, and a brace. With time and treatment, she will improve. She is lucky, they say.

"And so are we," Mom says on the drive back to the apartment. We left Dad reading the paper to Marni, with a promise to save him some pizza when he joins us later. But I hardly feel like eating tonight.

When Mom stops to pick up dinner, I wait in the car,

watching as she goes into the little Italian restaurant. Mom's squared shoulders sag just a little beneath her shirt, and her step is heavier. She comes back out empty-handed. "It's not ready yet," she says, sliding into the seat beside me with a sigh. And so we wait.

Suddenly it occurs to me I have not sat still with my mother since that day. She has been away this summer, having left in the worst kind of rush, the kind that makes you feel like the clothes will be torn from your body, your breath from your lungs. And now, here on this visit, we have still not recovered from that exit. The dust may have settled, but there has been so much debris beneath it to address. All of it Marni. Her recovery, her prognosis. It has been exhausting. I look at my mother, a rescue worker in her own right, unearthing every bit of good and holding it up to the light for her daughter, pressing it into her hands, with urgent insistence that all is well. Or will be.

I realize Mom has been doing this alone out here, for six weeks. Daddy and the Grands have come back and forth, and now, finally, me. But mostly it has been just her since that first day in the emergency room.

"Where is she?" Mom had cried when we roared into the emergency waiting area that afternoon in June. "I need to know if she's all right."

Dad didn't speak. He just paced the narrow hall leading to the ER doors. Up and down, up and down, a look of bewilderment on his face. But Mom stood sentinel, filling out paperwork, firing questions all the while, filling us in where Dad and I hovered in the corner. When Marni's friends began to arrive, they stood away from my mother as if from a wild animal. Finally the doctor called us in. They told us Marni was being admitted. She was having a CT scan. She was still unconscious. There were questions about the accident. How long was she underwater? Was she breathing on her own when she was pulled out? These were questions I could not answer. They were questions I should have been able to, had I been with her on the rock.

But Mom has never said as much to me. She has been too consumed with survival. Now, she leans back in the seat beside me, removes her sunglasses, and rubs her eyes. Then she grabs her purse, fiddling with her wallet, checking her cell phone. She taps the steering wheel, a nervous rhythm. Even now, at the day's end with an empty stomach, she is unable to idle.

I reach over and place my hand on hers, and she goes still. When we face each other, our eyes are dry and red and endless. I look into hers deeply, relieved that no tears press against my own. I cannot imagine where my mother's strength comes from, and I marvel silently at her as we hold hands and wait for the restaurant to deliver our pizza to the car window.

Goodbye

On my last night in Portland, I stay late at the hospital. Marni's long brown hair is no longer sun-streaked, but, like Gran says, it's still silk, and I sit behind her on the bed braiding it.

"That feels nice," she murmurs. That whole evening we watch TV and look at magazines. One of the nurses brings us Scrabble. Marni watches the letters spill across the board as I empty the box.

"You first," I say.

"You're tan," she says, examining my hand. "So you've been to the beach?"

"No, just the pool. To watch Beth Ann," I reply.

"Why?"

"Because she wanted me to."

"No, I mean why haven't you gone to the lake?"

I don't know what to say to this, so I concentrate on the game board.

"Is *booger* really a word?"

Marni ignores this. "Lace, I mean it. You love the water as much as I do. And you're good. You can't stop because of . . ." She gestures toward the sheets, toward her legs.

"I just don't want to," I say with a shrug.

"Are you afraid?" Marni's green eyes blaze. "Is that why you've stayed away?" She slaps the sheets.

I stand up quickly, move to the window, and then back. Marni never gets this mad.

"I don't know," I say, starting to cry.

"Well, I am!" she yells. Her voice is dark and trembly. "Every day, Lace. Every single day. I'm afraid I won't walk. Afraid I can't do this. I don't want to be here, but I'm afraid to go home. Don't you see? I'm afraid of so many things, Lace, so you can't be. You don't get to be afraid!"

Her eyes swell with tears and her hands shake. I sit down and grab them, press them against my lips.

"I'm sorry, Marni. I'm sorry I didn't jump with you."

She shakes her head angrily. "Stop it, Lace. Stop. It would've happened anyway. It could've happened to anyone that day."

"But it didn't happen to anyone. It happened to you!" I shout.

"Yeah, it did." She looks at me and cups my face firmly. "But it didn't happen to *you*."

Hot tears soak my shirt, and my nose runs with them. But I do not look away from her. I don't let my eyes leave hers. I wait and I look, searching for her blame. For her anger at my leaving her here alone. But there is none.

"I needed you," she says finally, her voice a soft whisper. "I wish you'd come sooner."

"I'm so sorry," I cry. It is worse, this leaving thing. Worse than causing accidents, worse than being scared. I thought she was better off if I stayed away, as if I were some kind of reminder of all that she had lost, and who caused it. I blamed myself. But in staying away I had done more harm. I realize now that staying away was a selfish act. I think of Beth Ann's freckled back turned away from me in the pool. I think of Sully Tanner's wide-eyed sadness on our porch. And I think of Willa Dodge, gliding through the midnight waters like some kind of spirit. I want to go home. And I want Marni to come with me.

"I just want things to be the same."

Marni nods, pushing her hair back, sitting up straight. "But they aren't."

I remember Sully's package then. I find my bag under the bed and rummage through until it crinkles against my fingers. It is small and wrapped in plain tissue paper.

"Here," I say as I pass it to Marni.

She turns it over in her hands. "What is it?"

"He came by the house."

She closes her eyes and presses the package to her chest before she opens it. Then she spills the contents onto the bed and gasps. A tiny pinecone rolls across the sheets. There are three white pebbles, perfectly round. And a yellow daisy, dried and pressed, its petals open like the sun. Marni holds these for a long time, her slender fingers moving across each item, turning them over and over in her pale hands. She is still bent over her treasures, the moon rising behind her in the window as I get up to leave.

"What did he send you?" I ask.

"The lake," she says. "He sent me the lake."

Midnight Invitation

On the first night of my return home, there is a gentle knock at my bedroom door. It's past midnight and the lake breeze whirls around my room.

"Come in," I whisper into the dark, but there is no response. Quietly I slide from my bed. I open the door just a crack and peer into the hall. But nobody's there. From downstairs I hear the screen door slap shut. Cinder comes up behind me and whines.

"What is it, boy?" Before I can stop him, he noses the door open. "Cinder, get back here!" He disappears downstairs.

As I step into the hall after him, I trip over something outside my door.

"What's this?" I feel in the darkness. There's a fuzzy towel with something wrapped inside. I scoop it up and return to my room, flicking on the light.

Inside the towel is a sleek new swimsuit. The beach

towel is our own, from the hall closet. I realize what this is. It's an invitation.

My stomach sinks with dread as I pull on the suit, but there's something else. Excitement? I turn out the lights. Dad wouldn't want me outside in the middle of the night. And I don't really want to go myself, but something pokes at me like a reminder. It's something I need to finish.

Outside the wind is stronger, but it's the warm wind of a balmy summer night. The trees sway, fragrant with pollen and pine, as I make my way down the porch stairs. Cinder waits, tail wagging, at the bottom, his whole body saying, "Let's go!" He takes off again, this time down the trail. Down to the lake.

I make my way over rocks and roots, careful not to trip. Cinder woofs ahead. When I get to the shore, the beach is empty. Where is she?

And then I see her. Wading in the water, up to her waist, is Willa Dodge. Cinder races in, splashing loudly against the quiet night.

"Cinder, no!" I hiss, but Willa doesn't seem to mind.

"Bad dog," she says with a small smile. "The water's warm tonight."

She's right. My toes curl into the sand as the water laps against them. Maybe I'll wade in just a little.

Willa lowers herself, her arms fanning the water in slow, gentle strokes. She moves out into the lake, and I watch as she disappears in the night. I stand at the shore, willing myself in, just one more step. But I can't.

Soon Willa circles back to shore, and when she emerges she joins me on the sand.

"It's nice out here now. No one to bother you. No questions to answer. Just you and the night." She pats herself with the towel, gazing up at the stars.

"You're a competitive swimmer?" I ask. My voice squeaks a little, not in fear but with shame.

"Used to be," she says. "I think I could swim before I could walk."

"Like Marni," I whisper. "I saw your trophies," I add, blushing in the dark.

She looks at me now. "So you did."

"You really won all those races?"

"Is that hard to believe?"

"I'm sorry, I thought . . . Well, I thought you were just a helper from the agency."

"Yes, dear, and a mother, and a retired nurse. And a slow old swimmer." This last part she says with a laugh. "I've been lots of things in this life."

And I knew none of them. I realize I don't even know Willa. Shame washes over me. I imagine it seeping into the sand, burning Willa's toes. I wonder if she knows.

"That suit fit you all right?"

"Yes, thank you," I tell her. "It's perfect." And it is. The water, the suit, the invitation. All of it, perfect. And yet I can't go in. Willa seems to understand.

"Well, it's getting late. Best get this body to bed," she says suddenly.

"Yeah, it *is* pretty late," I agree, fingering the strap of my suit. "I'd better try it out another time."

Willa looks up at the house. A light in her window illuminates the path back. "You know, it's not a good idea to be out here alone. But if someone knew where you were, and if someone knew to keep an ear open for you, your dad might not mind." She finishes toweling herself off carefully, facing the lake the whole time.

"Yeah, Dad does tend to worry."

She nods. "That's his job."

"And besides, I am pretty tired," I tell her, digging in the sand with my big toe. The lake laps it like a giant dog.

"Well, I'm not quite tired yet. In fact, I may stay up and read awhile." She looks at me. "You know, I like to leave the windows open when I read. I can hear and see the lake from my room."

"Really?" I set the towel down.

"Yeah, I kind of watch over it."

"Like a lifeguard?"

"More like a friend." She stands, gathering herself up with her belongings. "You coming, then?"

I study the water, thinking this over. "Maybe I'll sit awhile," I say. "The stars are pretty nice tonight."

"Sure are."

"And Cinder can keep me company."

"He sure can." Above us, her room glows warmly.

"And your light will be on?"

"Like a lighthouse," she says. And then she is gone, humming quietly to herself all the way up the path.

Into the Lake

I think of a Robert Frost poem our teacher read to us last winter. *The woods are lovely, dark and deep, but I have promises to keep.*

The lake, the sky, all of it is dark and deep. But not frightening. It's just me and the world for a while.

As for promises, I remember what Marni said. It didn't happen to me.

Just like I imagined, the water is warm as I wade in. Cinder circles twice, settling on the red towel. When I enter the lake, it is silent, as if it's holding its breath, as if it's been waiting for me all summer. One step, two, then three. The ground disappears beneath my feet as the water rises softly around me. It comes as a relief. Soon I am waist deep in the water, and the lake stretches out before me to the moon. I tip my head back, the water soaking my hair, streaming now down my back.

Tonight there will be two sets of wet tracks in the hallway, each leading to a different door. I wonder if Dad will notice in the morning. Over my shoulder, Willa's light glows steadily, faithful in the window. It is the last thing I see before I sink beneath the water, swallowing the night air as the lake gently swallows me.

Homecoming

It is late August, and our house is filled to bursting. Every quiet corner is noisy, every empty chair plucked from hiding has a rear end on it. Tables groan under the weight of food and flowers. Cinder keeps a quiet watch from under the coffee table, eyeing each guest who squeezes into the house. Each doorway has a shining new ramp now. The entryway to the house, the back porch, even the step up to the kitchen. Ramps are all over the house, and Grampa Martin has spent the better part of the week touching up the paint, smoothing the edges. Even now he crouches among the guests, fussing over them.

"They look good, Grampa," I tell him. He hands me his toolbox.

"Pass me a little sandpaper, will ya, Bean?"

A rolled piece of paper falls out onto the floor. I open it up.

"Don't lose that! That's the master plan," he says.

I recognize it immediately. It is the hand-sketched map of our house, the one from under Willa's bed, the entries and exits carefully marked and measured.

"Willa made this map," I say.

"Well, of course she did. How else do you think we put all this together? I couldn't have done it without her."

I look around the room, but Willa's nowhere to be found.

"Peach pies are out," Gran announces, inching through the kitchen crowd.

"Whoo-ee, Jemima!" Grampa hollers above the noise, as everyone cheers.

Across the house the doorbell keeps ringing, and even though no one can get through to answer it, it doesn't matter. People keep coming.

There's the swim team, and Sully, of course, hovering by the windows, looking up each time someone new enters, then returning to their animated conversations. Neighborhood families crowd around and onto couches. There are high school teachers arranging platters and policemen eyeing dessert trays. Dad's co-workers stand nervously on the perimeter, taking deep sips from coffee mugs.

Newcomers nod hello, waving and bobbing through the undulating sea of guests. Small children zigzag through, banging into grownup kneecaps. Dad and I stand on the bottom step, surveying the scene.

"I think we have a situation," he says happily. He checks his watch, the watch that is no longer missing since he found it stuck in one of his suitcase pockets, probably forgotten during a trip to Portland. "Should be any minute now."

The doorbell rings repeatedly until everyone is shouting, "Come in, come in." Eventually someone peeks around the door. There in the doorway is Beth Ann Watts, finally home from her family vacation, holding a crooked bouquet of something yellow. Probably daisies. She smiles uncertainly.

Willa appears and sweeps the door open wide. "Get a move on, chicken legs, the party's waiting."

Beth Ann nods nervously and hops through the doorway like she's leaping through a ring of fire. Willa's eyes fix on me on the stairs. She takes Beth Ann's hand, guiding her in, directing her through the crowd, to me. I rise and move toward her.

We meet in the middle of the family room. Beth Ann looks at the floor and pushes her glasses higher on her nose.

"I brought these," she says.

"Thanks," I say, taking the flowers. We both stare at our feet.

"Want some pie?" I ask.

"Peach?"

"You bet. Gran just made it."

"Well, okay. But is it organic?"

I start to laugh. It's just a little giggle, and I don't mean to hurt her feelings, but suddenly I'm so relieved I can't stop. It pours out. I laugh louder and longer, until my tummy strains and people turn to stare.

"What?" Beth Ann asks, fingering the wipes that I know are in her pocket. "What's so funny?"

"Nothing," I say, taking her hand. "Come on, the pie's in here. And yes, it's organic."

With all the noise and activity, no one has noticed the red van pulling up the front drive. Except for one. From under the coffee table there is a hearty *woof.* Heads turn as the table wobbles and the giant black dog streaks out from underneath, flashing through legs and over laps. As if on cue, Willa, still at her post, pulls the front door open, and Cinder sails through.

A strong breeze fills the room, and everybody raises their head to the wind. There is a hush. The smell of the lake fills the house, swirling among the guests, lapping at the tables. Bringing with it the scent of leaves, the late sun, and finally Marni herself. She fills the door, windblown and rosy. The sun reflects off the silver wheels of her chair, smattering the walls in a million tiny sparkles. She smiles shyly as Mom appears behind her wheelchair.

There is a collective pause, and the crowd shifts. And then someone in the back of the room claps. It spreads. The clapping washes over all of us, filling the house, pressing up against the ceiling. It rings through the walls of our home, to the trees and sky outside. Suddenly everyone is cheering and Dad is kneeling before her chair, pulling Marni into him, and Gran is cradling Mom in her arms like a baby. From nowhere Grampa throws me over his shoulder, and we wade toward them, through the crowd, through the wind, toward home.

Self-Portrait

Coming home doesn't make everything the same. I understand that now. It's not easy, but I am trying to get used to it. For a while things were quiet around here. Sully came by with Jennifer and Alex. At first they were timid and unsure, but Marni wasn't having any of that. Soon they were pushing her around the house, watching movies and fixing themselves snacks in our kitchen like the old days. Now Marni's other friends come to see her more, and she's even started going to the indoor pool at the high school again. After hours, when the pool is quiet, she and Willa work in the shallow end. Willa has her swimming already, using her upper body to pull herself through the water. It's pretty amazing. Dad cried the first time we went to watch.

During after-school practices, Marni sits on the pool deck and watches her team. She's getting so much stronger now, walking most of the day with her leg in a brace, balancing on her quad cane. Her walk is a bit lopsided and slow, something that caused others to stare at first. I'm sure Marni noticed, but she never said so. We're just so happy to see her up and out of the wheelchair more and more. And though we thought the swim practices would be hard for her to sit through, she insists on going. So Mom drives her back to school each afternoon, after her own physical therapy sessions are over. If Marni's really tired that day, she'll sit in her wheelchair with Sully at her side. Her friends line up beside her on the bench, comparing times and scrutinizing strokes. Sometimes even the boys come over and joke around with her like old times. The way they splash and carry on in front of her you'd think nothing's changed. But I don't give them all the credit. I think it has a lot more to do with the fact that it's Marni in that chair.

Fall is almost over. My sketchbook is full, full of all the colors and people and places of this past summer. I've drawn Gran in the kitchen, the counter beside her piled with pies and desserts. There's Grampa with his tools in his red truck, both coming and going. There are two of Dad. The earlier one is of him hunched over piles of paper in his office. The later one is outdoors, of us lying under the trees on the porch, our hands behind our heads. There's Beth Ann in the pool swimming away from me. And Willa at the window. Smiling.

Finally there is Marni. Home, with us again. Though she is not surrounded by family and friends. I didn't draw the big party. It's of her sitting in her wheelchair when she first got home looking out at the lake. Not sad, but peaceful. Like she's comfortable to sit beside it for a while.

Marni always knew who she was. She's not an artist, but if she drew a picture of herself it would be bright and full, no spot on the page left white. I think of my drawings, and how careful I used to be. How so much of the page was left unfilled, how the colors were soft and safe. When Marni's accident happened, her page didn't go blank. It was torn. And while she was in Portland mending the frays, I was only just beginning to fill in my own pages here at home. Trying out new colors, shading in the edges.

I used to wonder what I would tell Marni about Sully Tanner when she came back. About how he was my friend this summer. I don't think of him now as just the swim captain or my older sister's boyfriend. Now he's one of the colors on my page. Someday I'll tell her that.

For now I sketch the two of them, sitting out on the porch as the sun goes down. They are not alone. From where I sit there are three. On the left is Marni. There is the strong, elegant line of her neck, holding her head high. The chestnut hair swept across the back of her chair. On the right is Sully, perched close beside her on the bench. Leaning in, watching with so much love I don't think I can fit it on the page. And in the middle, there is the lake, glimmering in the distance. They hold hands, fingers bridging the water between them, as if they're trying to wrap their arms around it.

Today

Things are different now that it's winter. This fall Beth Ann became an official member of the Saybrook High junior varsity swim team. She finally competed in her first meet last week. She didn't exactly win, but she surprised us all by coming in fourth place. It was the crawl. Now she says she's working on her butterfly. It's not pretty to watch, but her time isn't so bad. Coach says she's really coming along. In fact, she awarded her the most improved swimmer award at the end-of-season banquet. The way Beth Ann blushed and grinned you would've thought she won the Olympic gold. Who knows? Maybe next season Beth Ann Watts will be the girl to beat.

My times are improving, too. Coach has been helping me with my stroke, sending me into the pool every day. At our last meet she sat right behind the blocks with my parents, a voice in my head right up until the gun sounded.

"Head down, Lace. Hold it, hold it." The voice I hear underwater and in my dreams. I guess that's just the way it is when the coach is your sister.

In the end, last summer was a summer like no other. And so none of us was surprised when it lasted well into fall, the temperatures almost balmy until the first week of October. The boats stayed moored, the docks remained in the water. Even the birds seemed to linger on the shores in confusion. And so, before summer finally gave in to fall, I held on to my midnight swims. Each night there'd be two sets of footprints down the hall, mine and Willa's. We'd swim alongside each other real quiet, or pass one another on the path. There wasn't anything to talk about. Like she said, midnight swims are the healing ones. And so there was no way I could keep them all for myself anymore. They just weren't mine to hold on to.

Soon there was just one set of footprints in our hall. But it stopped at two doors. It started at the top of the stairs, where it veered left, the fresh, wet tracks leading right up to Marni's room. Then it retraced back down the hall, past my own door, and ended at Willa's. The footprints were almost dry by the time they got there.

I never asked about it. I knew it was as it should be. One night I opened my window to see. The breeze swirled around my room, rustling my curtains, tickling my face. It filled up my room, the damp, earthy scent of leaves and lake. Of sun and sand and rain. Outside, the lake was all lit up. I saw them there. The strong, stout figure of Willa Dodge, carrying her charge carefully down the rocky path to the shore, cradling her. They eased into the water, slowly, as one. Willa held on to her until they'd waded in, the lake settling itself around the two of them.

Marni perched above the watery world in Willa's arms. I held my breath. Then Willa lowered her in, setting Marni free. A pale slip against the dark, returning to the lake, where tiny spirals danced as she pierced the water, welcoming her back like a whisper in the waves.

Acknowledgments

This story would not be here to be shared without the help and guidance of so many good people who assisted me along the path.

First, a tremendous thank-you to Dr. Alyse B. Sicklick, M.D., the attending physiatrist and Rehabilitation Division medical director of Gaylord Hospital in Wallingford, Connecticut. Dr. Sicklick was more than generous with her time, expertise, and enthusiasm as I worked to make Marni's story as authentic as possible. I am most grateful to her for inviting me to Gaylord and allowing me to peer into the window of a traumatic brain injury patient's rehabilitative experience. I applaud the families and patients of Gaylord for their bravery and perseverance. Meeting them was an overwhelming experience that touched this writer far beyond the pages of her book.

Thank you, also, to Carrie Kramer, MA, CRC, the advocacy and community relations director of BIAC, the Brain Injury Association of Connecticut. She pointed me in Dr. Sicklick's direction, referred me to invaluable resources, and shared her personal experience as well. I was touched by the gratitude of all the experts I spoke with as they cheered my efforts to bring brain injury education to light.

My sincere thanks to fellow author Michael Paul Mason, writer of *Head Cases: Stories of Brain Injury and Its Aftermath*. Michael patiently lifted the veil of TBI and helped me to understand the medical and personal implications for its patients. His kind correspondence was as technical as it was generous, and I am so grateful for his expertise and encouragement.

Thanks to Janine O'Malley, my editor at FSG, who once again led me to the light at the end of the tunnel. The second time around you were just as gracious and supportive, an archer of an editor, who shows me the bull's-eye every time.

Thank you to my agent, Barbara Markowitz, who fills my mailbox with marketing ideas and my head with encouraging words. She keeps me ever mindful of the next step.

This book has to be for Rush, the greatest dog a girl could have, who curled up at my feet (or on the bed!) for every page of this book. As with most things in life, the journey was made richer by the company of a good dog. To *mes bonnes amies*, Jennifer, Sarah, and Alex, who remind me every day that I need to do this. I love you for believing so deeply in me and reminding me to do the same. I am also grateful for the little slice of Heaven

known as Sherman, a town that has shown such enthusiasm to this resident writer. I owe much to my family, to
my loving parents, Marlene and Barry Roberts, who first
introduced me to the natural world and the love of a good
story, two elements that make me put pen to paper. To
Jason, who loved this story best from the start and cried in
all the right places. (He still thinks he's the one who came
up with this title, and I'll let him believe that for a little
while longer.) Finally, to my girls, Finley and Gracie, who
will always come first, and for whom I make this promise
every single day. I love you all. To the moon and back.